PASTORAL COUNSELLING

PASTORAL COUNSELLING

Edison Y.M.

2011

Pastoral Counselling – Published by the Rev. Dr. Ashish Amos of Indian Society for Promoting Christian Knowledge (ISPCK), Post Box 1585, 1654 Madarsa Road, Kashmere Gate, Delhi-110006.

© Author, 2011

ISBN: 978-81-8465-128-7

Laser typeset by **ISPCK,** Post Box 1585,
1654 Madarsa Road, Kashmere Gate, Delhi-110006
Tel: 23866322, 23866323
e-mail–ashish@ispck.org.in   • ella@ispck.org.in
website-www.ispck.org.

Dedicated to
my dear loving father

CONTENTS

viii

ACKNOWLEDGEMENTS

At first, I humbly thank God the almighty Father. He helped me to translate with joy and enthusiasm His inner promptings eventually leading me to realize one of my aspirations and dreams. Drawing from my vast reading, the laborious research I did, now appears as a book, "Pastoral Counselling", published as an easy beckoner for all who would avail themselves of it. Praise God!

I also devotedly remember with filial affection, our Archbishop the Most Rev. Dr. Soosa Pakiam M., for his blessings, support and encouragement in my priestly ministry. For the "Foreword" to this maiden venture of mine, I am truly indebted to His Grace.

I have received invaluable help from Sister M. Laetitia CCR., my teacher at the seminary. She has gone meticulously through the text. To say the least she has done a wonderful job which can never be forgotten.

I would like to express my sincere gratitude to all the professors at the Pontifical Institute, Alwaye. I extend my deep thanks to Fr. Xavier Kattikatt OSA for his guidance and timely assistance in my need.

To Brother Anish Ouseph who was there by my side all along, and to Sumesh Martin for the attractive cover imaging, my prayerful and sincere thanks.

To Rev. Dr. Ashish Amos, General Secretary, ISPCK and the editorial Board of ISPCK, Delhi, I am indeed grateful for the layout, printing and publication of this work.

Special thanks to my well wishers and friends to the priests of Trivandrum, my parents and siblings.

In conclusion I must say that I have quoted authorities and acknowledged sources quite liberally.

While writing this book I found there all the challenges and responsibilities, pitfalls and demands a counsellor faces. The book provides the reader with information, insights and keys for nurturing the counsellor within him. It aims at stimulating anyone directly involved in counselling or any one who may be called to it.

The counsellor cannot simply be a person who is well informed about the problematic issues besetting the information - heavy age that we presently live in. Counselling is an additional and most accurate basic need of people today. To meet it, the counsellor needs to find in the Incarnate Word Jesus, the source for his words of advice and guidance. If "Pastoral Counselling" should appeal as a how to do it guide, I am happy.

1st June, 2011   **Fr. Edison Y.M.**

FOREWORD

It is encouraging and a pleasure to write the Foreword to "Pastoral Counselling" a ministerial endeavour of Fr. Edison Y.M. Counselling is defined as a helping relationship in which the counsellor understands his client and leads him to a better life situation. As pastors the clergy is engaged in the counselling ministry.

Fr. Edison Y.M. elaborates on the need of this helping relationship. The present day life situations are fraught with much stress. People with high expectations but with low potential feel so inadequate and helpless that counselling has indeed become a need. The priest has to face challenges and interact with people who undergo varying emotions that range from joy to sorrow, from anger to grief. He can be a congruent and effective counsellor only if he knows the art of counselling, as well, as he knows himself.

The author has drawn meaningfully from the Scriptures and is committed to the practical application of the numerous therapies and techniques he cites, and the psychological theories and methods he blends in the light of faith.

Reflecting on the future of pastoral counselling I am personally convinced that although there are as yet no established patterns and processes outlined, it needs to be a theological leadership enriched by a deep spiritual formation involving the whole person - body, mind and soul. For this to materialize, very much has to be done in the seminaries for priestly formation. Imparting mere intellectual training will not suffice. Our seminaries have to be centers for training in true discernment of the signs of the times.

The priest who is in person another Christ, must have the capacity to lead others to Christ, "The Way, the Truth and the Life". Fr. Edison paves the way towards becoming and being light.

Fr. Edison has also offered a list of books for the further reading of sources for those seeking what he has found useful. "Pastoral Counselling" deserves a wide readership. I recommend it as a rich treasure trove for counsellors, religious, the clergy, teachers, seminarians, even for lay persons who are interested in the art of counselling.

At present this publication may be a small step which however, I hope will eventually lead the author to take a giant leap in the field of counselling. While congratulating Fr. Edison on this excellent work I wish him success in all his future enterprises and invoke God's abundant blessings on him.

Most Rev. Dr. Soosa Pakiam M.
Metropolitan Archbishop of Trivandrum

INTRODUCTION

Going by WHO, it is estimated that by 2020, the disability due to mental disorders will be the highest in the world. In other words, disability due to mental disorders will be much more than disability due to heart attack and cancer. Among mental disorders, depression conduces to disability to the maximum. At a global level the prevalence of mental disorders is increasing in an alarming and unprecedented manner among adolescents and senior citizens. The third major reason for death among adolescents is suicide, domestic violence, alcoholism and drug abuse, which are increasingly going unchecked.

The Indian scenario is also a reflection of this global trend of mental ill health. When it pertains to the narrow strip of land called Kerala we get a significantly magnified malignancy of mental health problems. In all parameters it goes much beyond the statistical number games. Though Kerala is often labelled as *God's own country*, it has the highest consumption of psychiatric drugs, per capita consumption of alcohol; domestic violence is also highest. What is more, suicide rates the highest in Kerala for the 13th time. Hence today Kerala is dubbed as the suicidal capital of India, but the slogan for tourism promotion is still *God's own country*. A bird's eye view of mental health facts and figures, sad to say indicate that in reality Kerala has metamorphosed into *devils' country*.

An analysis of this anatomy reveals that the root cause of all these problems cannot be treated to biochemical abnormality within the brain. Rather no brain exists and is expressed in a psychological vacuum. In the pathological changes in the equation of the social fabric with its penetration into the web of relationships of shattered family ties, broken family structures and alienated human existence, what surfaces is the hallmark of mental health hazards, a reflection on social pathology, designed and developed by micro structures across the globe controlled by remote fiscal policies and social philosophies.

Religion in the context of social institutions has a pivotal role in preserving the delicate balance between society and man. Pastoral practices acquire a new dimension of meaning with *logotherapy* and other scientifically developed and tested therapies, tools, and techniques commonly called for in counselling.

A scrutiny and scan of the religious practices of counselling reveals that the current status is far from satisfactory. There is certainly a felt need for adding a new dimension to the art and science of counselling. In this venture, Fr. Edison YM has essentially contributed to fulfilling the time felt need for the perspective building process by drafting a monograph. This work is small in volume; but rich in content. Ranging from the history of pastoral counselling and counselling in general, it gives us a kaleidoscopic vision of principles, practices, tools, and theories of counselling and without however, compromising the art and science of counselling, it keeps the spirit of the procedures at its zenith. Perhaps "Pastoral

Counselling" is a window to peep through for procedures of counselling, for acquiring the right equation of knowledge, skills and attitudes for equipping the clergy to deliver this service.

Dr. K. Gireesh
President, Indian Association of
Clinical Psychologists

I. THE RELEVANCE

Jesus is *the Counsellor*. There are scriptural references that underscore the importance of counselling. "And his name will be called Wonderful Counsellor" (Isaiah 9,6). "Where there is no guidance, a people falls; but in an abundance of counsellors there is safety"(Proverbs 11,14). The Parish priest, an *alter Christus*, is also called to share in the work of Christ, as a counsellor.

Counselling is a felt need today. From a psychological perspective this age is one of stress and anxiety. High expectations, burdensome tasks, mounting personal responsibilities, prestige maintenance and liabilities as such all these frustrate a person. Besides, there is little time for leisure and quiet. People do not normally highlight their positive aspects and achievements; they tend rather to focus on their negativity and failures. They step up negative emotions, and are prone to react easily with anger, jealousy, hatred, fear etc. getting the better of them. Their sensitivity towards persons and things and their consequent sudden responses bring in their wake many other problems like broken relationships, loss of career opportunities and the like.

Furthermore, man is born and brought up in an ambience of relationships. Max Weber defines society 'as a web of relationships'. Nobody can lead an isolated life, since one needs the help and care of the other in one-way or another. Though one is a part of groups like the family, Church, school, college, firm etc. the great misfortune of our time is the break up of relationships and disinterestedness in building and forging relationships. People lead anonymous lives in the home and family ties are severed. Parents are often interested in their own pursuits and the children follow suit. Mutual love and care being the soul of the family its absence makes family life a hell, where nobody wants to communicate except to satisfy primary needs.

People prefer to remain isolated. The option for the flat system is a striking proof. The neighbour is scarcely befriended. A chance meeting of a neighbour entails a forced social smile, very easy substitute for even a simple greeting. The truth is that people do not want others to interfere in their family affairs. This leaves them free to make a show and boast of high living despite their real financial status. There is reluctance and resistance even in restoring broken family relationships. Here pride will not give way to humility. People divided on sectarian grounds like geography, money, power, education and vested interests do great harm to the development of a community. In a parish such groups give counter witness in comparison to healthy youth groups, pious associations, parish communities etc. Making them aware of the lacunae is a laborious and time consuming issue when there are other social problems like the dowry system, unemployment, suicidal tendencies, alcoholism, drug addiction etc which certainly claim the special attention of the pastor.

Cultural issues also add to the pastoral problems. The fast growing media especially the TV and Internet have bad effects on children. The media highlights sex as the only focal point of life. The adverse vision of life and the lurid pictures incite the young minds and cause untold harm to society and individuals. The effects of globalisation and cultural implantation though good in themselves often highlight the bad effects which are reflected in our society. Literature, music, dance, and cinema are all caught up and not free from the fetters of bad influence. Hence a moral and cultural awakening is an essential need of the time. In the final analysis, in their anxiety to make a living people forget their priorities. So a mega project has to be charted out for resolving cultural and moral issues.

Likewise in the political and educational arenas the situation is quite deplorable. Politicians do not have backbones and they easily forget traditionally prized values. Conscientizing them is not very easy, as many of the politicians do not come within the spectrum of the Church. In such a situation counsellors could guide the minor groups of Christian leaders by inculcating and upholding values and imparting the correct vision of life. Education is today becoming a commercialised product. There are many Christian institutions that sell education at exorbitant rates. In many places the parish priest is the local manager of the school. Parish priests could certainly implement value education in the initial stages.

Human life is currently becoming more complex with the fast advancing trends of consumerism, globalisation, cyber technology etc. Often one has to face problems and even tragedies in life. The newspapers publish reports of deaths, murders or suicide, family problems, sex issues, drug addictions etc. Our parishes are also fettered by these chains. The wounded mind is the fertile breeding ground for all these types of problems. The disintegrated, unrealistic, unfulfilled self and identity crisis do not promote growth and self actualisation or self transcendence.

Priests are the leaders of the church community, and a priest who is empowered to lead people to God is also responsible for these issues. As a pastoral counsellor the minister needs a unique understanding of his own self image, role, functions, and goals. His self-understanding must spring from a theological basis derived from his awareness of the grounding of what he does in ongoing life, the message and tradition of the Church. Jesus did his ministry as an integrated liberator and healer of both the physic and the psyche. The emphasis of Vatican II on the priesthood and its shift from the cultic priesthood to a more humane, people-oriented, serving nature makes this task easier. At present many priests are engaged in pastoral counselling on their own initiative though it is regrettable that the time to have got things organized is long overdue.

Religion and psychology are not two distinct disciplines, since the mind and body are related, and share a reciprocal relationship. Priests could use various psychological methods to help the souls in pastoral counselling and guide them to God. The medieval missionary yearning for saving souls is reiterated today in the mitigation of souls. Pastoral Counselling is a precious, holistic, timely and relevant means for the wellbeing of man. A priest can communicate healing messages to people who are struggling in alienation or despair. Thus pastoral counselling is concerned with lifesaving action in general.

Pastoral counselling contributes to the renewal of the Church by providing an instrument for the renewal of persons, groups and relationships. It helps one to be the Church, the community in which God's love becomes an experienced reality in relationship. Thus pastoral counselling is an instrument of renewal through reconciliation: reconciliation with one's self, others, and with the cosmos. It could be an instrument of renewal by helping one to develop what is most difficult to achieve in the history of relationships. The realism of consumerist culture illustrates the use and throw-away model, while, Globalisation has neither any concern for values nor relations but for profit at any cost.

Ministers are perceived as representatives of the Christian Church. This means that some people avoid approaching them despite their lone struggle with personal problems. The reason for this is quite varied and is associated with their idiosyncratic response to the symbolic role of the clergy. Many adults continue to see the clergy through the eyes of their childhood days, possibly recalling judgemental or punitive encounters with strict and intimidating religious authority figures.

Pastoral counselling in the Indian context is at work in an informal way, in contrast to that of the US, where many priests spend most of their time in this ministry. The need for a formal counselling set-up is obvious. Priests and seminarians should be well trained for this purpose. Theology and Philosophy, which are the two disciplines of the mind, are manifested through prayer and behaviour. Theological guidelines to help the mind by using psychological approaches are to be further developed in the arena of psychology and religion, and religious psychology. Formal counselling could be given through appointment, which seeks the availability of the priest. The availability of the priest is another contending factor. Some priests are unaware of time management and often least concerned about their parishes. This lack of care and inattention paves the way for the dropouts from Catholicism for settlements in Pentecostal Churches. However one has yet to meet people thirsting for counselling. There are many people going to simple, ordinary lay counsellors at the Charismatic Centres. People are overwhelmed with problems and finding no way to unburden themselves, they are disturbed, frustrated and the sad consequences are evident in society, working places, family, and in their relationships. Interpersonal relationships as such do not exist. Friends are only for a show, and are around for a past time. Siblings don't have sound relationships, and rarely do they even share sweets. The parents are burdened with their employment and daily family problems. In this set up there is nobody that understands and guides the other. Families and institutions are OK when viewed from the periphery but at the core, the condition is pitiable. The Church of India has a major role to play at this juncture as a moral guide and a policy maker. It is imperative that the Church in India realises the emerging needs of the people and finds the means to satisfy them.

There are many Charismatic Centres that deserve credit for the spiritual awakening of the Indian Church. They have contributed much in solving deep-seated family problems and addictions to drinks and drugs. They have brought personal comfort through a renewal of prayer life, reconciliation, and a fostering of a healthy vision of life. But the counselling they provide is rather defective. The counsellors with their inadequate training advise the retreatants superficially. They do not go deep into a person's problems and for the greater part such counselling has proved ineffective. There are some good counsellors who have the necessary expertise in the art of counselling.

There are various methods that could be used in pastoral counselling; to begin with the traditional psychoanalysis to the twenty minutes brief-therapy which includes the humanistic, existential or spiritual. For many years various methods were practised and some were found more effective. But which are the more effective ones is a question yet to be satisfactorily answered. If choosing the correct approach for each case is a laborious task, finding an approach for all cases is also impossible. In the pastoral setting priests can spend long hours over each case, but this would eliminate someone who needs more urgent help and this also to the detriment of the priest's daily ministry that needs to be attended to.

The aim of this work is to find out the various methods used in pastoral counselling and select the best approach that suits most of the cases. This attempt could be of great help for the researcher, and others to get an integral overall view of therapies as well as some specific therapies best suited to the Indian setup.

Jesus is the healer of humanity. The therapeutic healing of Jesus is different from that of others. His physical healings included not only the cure of the body but of the mind too. All sicknesses and pains can be traced to the infirmity of the mind. The mind gets distracted and frustrated because of the stress and strain of life. Anxiety and tension cause hypertension, cardiac arrest, peptic ulcers, asthma, eczema, and even certain cancers. Many cases, recorded as incurable in medical science have however been healed through the power of the mind and prayer. Hopefully pastoral counselling can also be better used in this perspective in physical healing. "I came that you may have life, and have it abundantly" (John 10, 10). And a Christian desires 'to be transformed by the renewal of the Pastor's mind.

II. FOUNDATIONS

A Definition

Carl R. Rogers describes the counselling process in the following words, "...the counsellor chooses to act consistently upon the hypothesis that the individual has a sufficient capacity to deal constructively with all those aspects of his which can potentially come into conscious awareness. This means the creation of an interpersonal situation in which the material comes into the client's awareness, and a meaningful demonstration of the counsellor's acceptance of the client as a person who is competent to direct himself." A workable definition of counselling is given by C.H. Patterson, "Counselling is a special kind of relationship between a person who asks for help with a psychological problem and a person who is trained to provide that help." But pastoral counselling is a helping relationship in which the counsellor is a priest. Michael J. O'Brien defines pastoral counselling as "a way of proceeding in an interpersonal relationship between a priest and a client, which seeks to free the client's capacity to live more fully as a child of God than he does presently, with greater openness to reality and inner harmony". Hiltner defines pastoral counselling, "as a process, which consists of a relationship between the pastor and parishioner not only at a given moment of time but as what happens within that relationship over a time span."

Pastoral counselling could also be termed as pastoral psychotherapy. If so, pastoral psychotherapy is the practice of psychotherapy in the context of a pastoral function and perspective. Pastoral psychotherapy is a kind of conversation, a kind of theologising in which the participants are understood to have multiple identities, experiencing and interpreting in interdisciplinary ways. In this conversation, the pastoral clinician faithfully companions and collaboratively translates with the client. It is a relationship in which persons tolerate ambiguities, and articulate and respond to ongoing questions with the hope of future understanding. The theological aspect is very much emphasised in pastoral counselling, which is also reflected in the definition of The Constitution of American Association of Pastoral Counselling (AAPC) namely, "exploration, clarification and guidance of human life, both individual and corporate, at the experiential and behavioural levels through a theological perspective." AAPC defines Pastoral Counselling as " a process in which a pastor utilizes insights and principles derived from the disciplines of theology and the behavioural sciences in working with individuals, couples, families, groups, and social systems toward the achievement of wholeness and health".

The distinctive feature of pastoral counselling is the inclusion of the religious dimension. According to Father Curran, "Pastoral counselling is a unique kind of relationship between the person and the counsellor, a relationship which implies and introduces God as a third party." There are some who stress the psychological aspects in pastoral counselling while others stress the spiritual aspect. Paul Huss sees it as a spiritual entity alone and calls pastoral counselling "Soulology". But a middle ground is more suitable in this context, as Robert

Wicks defines pastoral counselling as, "a focus on a person's relationship with the self and others with an eye to the influence God has in everyday life."

Pastoral counselling involves the life of the Spirit in each of its three functions, namely, the moral, cultural and religious function. It is an important and distinctive field within a field in which the participation of the Spirit is acknowledged, clarified and enabled. Thus pastoral counselling does not reduce the spiritual to psychology or spirituality alone. "There is a fundamental inter-dependency between the psychological and spiritual process taking place within persons and considers the spiritual dimension as the fabric of authentic life."

There are others like Vaughan, who say pastoral counselling is neither pastoral conversation, nor spiritual direction, nor psychological counselling or psychotherapy, nor just giving advice, nor just analysing the problem, but something more than that and may include the above-mentioned aspects. So he defines pastoral counselling " as a dialogue in which the counsellor establishes a relationship and attempts to assist another in bringing about changes in his/her way of living, solving or simply feeling supported by a caring person who represents the Church, all of which is done in the context of the individual's Christian faith and values." Dealing with adolescents and youth, Shelton defines pastoral counselling "as an encounter wherein the adult and adolescent/ young adult collaborate to reflect upon personal experiences, issues and attitudes in the young person's life. The fruits of this dialogue in turn lead the young person to gain deepening self-insights into his or her response to the

Lord, ongoing awareness of significant values and a growing capacity to make a healthy moral choice."

A suitable definition of pastoral counselling is seen in David G. Benner's suggestion: "pastoral counselling involves the establishment of a time-limited relationship that is structured to provide comfort for troubled persons by enhancing their awareness of God's grace and faithful presence and thereby increasing their ability to live more fully in the light of these realizations."

A Historical Note

Before entering into the modern history of pastoral counselling, a look through the Bible is essential. The nature and function of counselling is recognisable in the Scriptures. The religious counsellor was an integral part of the early Israelite courts, and in the Christian Bible, the notion of counsellor was even used to characterize the activity of the Holy Spirit.

In Exodus, Jethro advised Moses to appoint helpers to share in the work of counselling the people, and so lighten the burden (Exodus 18,1-2). Deuteronomy gives a sound account of the wise counsellors in Israel, who were also called Judges (Dt 25,5-10).

Jesus presents many examples of counselling; with the Samaritan woman at the well (John 4), with the sinful woman (John 8,1-11), with Zaccheus (Luke 19,1-10) and with Simon the Pharisee (Luke 7,36-50).

In many of the letters of Paul one finds references to his counselling: comforting (2 Cor 1,3-11), instructing and correcting (Acts 20,31) warning and teaching (Col 1,28).

A specific date to note in the history of pastoral counselling is impossible. William James' classical work,

The Varieties of Religious Experience: A Study of Human Nature (Cambridge, Mass., 1902/1985), provided one of the bases for the subject of the psychological study of religion to gain acceptance into the curricula of theological schools, particularly in American Protestant seminaries. In the beginnings of a pastor's care, there is a manner of dealing with the person with that unity of soul and body to which 'soul' refers in an extended sense. But pastoral counselling developed an identity separate from spiritual direction because of the acceptance of psychological and psychiatric theories within Catholicism. The broadening vision of the Church paved the way for considering psychology as a major subject in seminaries. In his *History of Pastoral Care in America* (1983), Holifield dates its development to the first decade of the twentieth century when a group of New England pastors first began to consider how the Church could put the newly developed procedures of psychotherapy into spiritual use. During this period the West was well on its way toward what Rieff has called the "triumph of the therapeutic" (Reiff 1966), and since the time when pastoral counselling emerged in its mature form in the 1940s and 1950s, it has often resembled, modern psychotherapy even more than the procedures historically associated with spiritual guidance. In a strict sense the pastoral counselling movement was founded in 1951 by Anton Boisen. He coined the phrase "the living human document" as a focus of study and care, and he was one of the first to attempt to introduce a psychological perspective into theological education and to challenge the strictly classical type of education found in most seminaries at the turn of the century. The practical orientation of the psychology of religion was expressed in the rise of this movement.

In Roman Catholicism counselling celebrated a successful achievement with Father Charles A. Curran a student of Rogers, who employed Thomostic philosophical categories to explain client-centered therapy in his *Counselling in Catholic Education* (1952). There are many others who interestingly made attempts in this field of pastoral counselling which remain closely associated to formal parishes and educational settings in Catholic tradition. Seward Hiltner, frequently considered as the Father of contemporary pastoral theology, was a strong critic of pastoral counselling whenever it appeared to over identify with the psychological and psychiatric theories and practices of the day. Other significant pioneers in the development of pastoral counselling were Wayne Oates, Paul E. Johnson, Carroll Wise, Howard Clinebell, and John Patton.

The history of salvation is the root of theology, that later affirms the historical Jesus as the messiah, the anointed one, which constituted the early faith and kerigmatic proclamation in Christianity. So a vignette on theology in relation to pastoral counselling is an unavoidable phenomenon.

Theology and Pastoral Counselling

The classical definition of theology is 'faith seeking understanding.' Understanding is what one lacks, thus causing problems in life. Theology is the human critical praxis of interdisciplinary conversation especially in the ever-present territory of the big questions, interpreted especially through the concepts of metaphor and narrative. The questions raised reach a point where they no longer speak, yet they communicate nonetheless. This is theology.

There is a possibility of theology being separated from pastoral identity and practice, because of one's faulty understanding of theology that leads to clinical problems later. Theologising is not *theoria,* speculative life but praxis, practical life, and it is the practice of "doing" theology. For Quintin Heads "Pastoral counselling is the practice of theology. For this praxis one needs both knowing theology and 'doing' theology." Schlauch proposes metaphor and narrative as natural bridges for the process of theologising. *Metaphor* is "understanding and exercising one kind of thing in terms of another," that is understanding the unfamiliar in terms of the familiar e.g. to say that "God is love" is to understand and experience God in terms of love. E.M. Foster defines " A story is a *narrative* of events arranged in a time sequence; we read on in a story to find out 'what happens next?' Persons live within stories and clinical praxis is, working in narratives, with pastoral counsellors as listeners and interpreters of stories.

Schlauch's idea of combining theology and psychology is an interdisciplinary approach in pastoral counselling. If pastoral counselling is essentially interdisciplinary, then pastoral counsellors must learn to become "bilingual" (Lindbeck, 1984). They must learn to be skilled in the language of the symbol system of theology as they are in that of psychology. These two perspectives are understood as offering categories of perception and discernment in the counselling situation.

Hunsinger gives a vivid account of Karl Barth's contributions to pastoral counselling. When pastoral counselling is understood as a ministry of the church, Barth is promising largely because the interdisciplinary dialogue he offers is intended as a theology of the Church.

Barth sees theology as grounded solely in God's self-revelation in Jesus Christ. He offers pastoral counsellors a perspective that is significantly designated to psychological modes of thought and can, therefore, help them to gain what Thomas Oden terms "sharpened kerigmatic identity." But according to Jennings a clear and distinct theological profile in interdisciplinary dialogue should not reduce different resources to a table of equivalence as neurosis = sin, wholeness = salvation or acceptance = justification etc...

Barthian insights for pastoral counselling are analysed by Shirley Gutherie from a Trinitarian and Christian Anthropological perspective.

Barth's methodological procedure of basing his theological anthropology is on the doctrine of the Trinity. Following this method, Gutherie outlines a Christian doctrine of the human person on the basis of a doctrine of the triune God. Human beings are thus understood from a threefold perspective; first as created in the image of God (derived from knowledge of God the Creator); second, as sinners who fail to live out God's purpose and who stand in need of redemption (derived from knowledge of Christ, the Redeemer); and third, as people who are promised a new humanity in Christ (derived from the knowledge of the Holy Spirit). In applying this Trinitarian anthropology to current questions in pastoral counselling, Gutherie deftly wends his way through a complex set of issues about the counsellor's attitude toward the physical body and human emotions. Gutherie sees the Christian pastoral counsellor working toward a goal in which "body, heart, mind and will are understood in their integrated relationship to each other". Human beings are not sinful by nature. Although fallen, human beings were created well, in the image of God the creator. Our real humanity is also affirmed in the real man, Jesus, who lived in thankful obedience to God. Sin is thus 'unreality,' self-contradiction. Pastoral counsellors can thus encourage their counselees to become their authentically human selves when they understand that to mean the humanity created, redeemed, and promised by God and hence the 'contradiction of the self-contradiction in which all human beings live.'

Gutherie concludes the study on Barth by directing the thoughts to grace and God's love. When pastoral counsellors are clear about these theological distinctions, they can better help their counselees to avoid both the Scylla of self-hatred and the Charybdis of moral laxity. Thus pastoral counsellors as ministers of the gospel stand for some thing distinctive.

"Pastoral" in Pastoral Counselling

If pastoral counselling is to be distinctively pastoral it must be returned to its proper place within pastoral care, which in turn must be understood in relation to the overall responsibilities of pastoral ministry. Pastoral ministry is not reducible to pastoral care. Pastoral ministry, the broadest context of pastoral counselling includes the following functions: preaching, teaching, leading worship, congregational leadership and administration, lay enabling, and pastoral care and counselling (Clinebell 1984). Pastoral counselling must, therefore, be conducted in a way that minimizes conflict with these other pastoral roles.

Pastoral counselling is also an activity of pastoral care, though it differs from other pastoral-care activities in several ways. Whereas the pastor can appropriately initiate a relationship of pastoral care, the parishioner usually initiates pastoral counselling. Furthermore, pastoral counselling has typically more of a problem focus, that is, something in the life or experience of the parishioner that is problematic and for which he or she seeks help. Whereas finally, in other pastoral-care activities, biblical precepts are immediately brought appropriately into the relationship by the pastor, in pastoral counselling the use of the Bible is usually not appropriate until the pastor has heard the parishioner's story.

Pastoral counselling and pastoral theology have common ground for agreements and disagreements. Theology can be well understood as 'faith seeking understanding'. It is taking the gospel into the living conditions of the people. And pastoral theology has a close relation to pastoral ministry and pastoral care, since they have their basis in it. The question that pastoral counselling raises for pastoral theology concerns the extent to which the specific experience of individuals shapes theological reflection. And many pastoral counsellors give greater importance to the voice of the individual experience than to the voice of theological reflection. They are more aware of the pain and sufferings that can be caused by abstract doctrinal or moral statements. So pastoral counselling generates the insight that meaningful and authentic existence arises first and foremost out of an honest engagement with one's personal experience. While on the other hand, there are some theologians arguing, that if pastoral counselling is to be as appointment form of pastoral practice arising out of the life and faith of the Church, then it needs to be substantially grounded in theological tradition.

Pastoral counselling is to be understood differently from Christian counselling. An erosion of the appropriate boundary between pastoral counselling and other forms of Christian counselling has not merely been the result of the clergy drifting from the pastoral role to that of psychotherapists. Of those describing themselves as Christian counsellors, very few are clerics; the movement is almost entirely associated with Christian mental-health professionals who seek to integrate their Christian values and counselling practice. Pastoral counselling is different from generic Christian counselling because the pastor who counsels is much more than a counsellor. Pastors relate to those they serve in counselling in a great variety of other ways, each reflecting one facet of the broad spectrum of pastoral responsibilities. Unlike the clinical counsellor, whether Christian or of the other faiths, the pastoral counsellor does not have the option of restricting contact with those seen in the scheduled counselling sessions. The pastor who counsels also engages with parishioners from the pulpit, in communities, at congregational fellowship events, and at the door after Church on Sunday mornings. Even if a pastor's sole responsibility is counselling, this counselling is a pastoral responsibility and is offered as part of the context of pastoral care.

Various models have emerged for pastoral care and counselling. Applying Erickson's life-cycle theory, David Capps (1983) developed a new pastoral care model that assigns three major roles to the clergy: that of moral counsellor, ritual co-ordinator and pastoral comforter. The uniqueness of the pastoral counselling can be understood from the nature of the pastoral counsellor and his functions.

'Counselling' in Pastoral Counselling

The term pastoral counselling and psychotherapy are both widely used often more or less interchangeably. Rogers views these two terms interchangeably because they appear to refer to the same basic method, which involves a series of direct contacts with the individual and aims to offer assistance in changing his attitudes and behaviour. But Bordin (1955) and Mowrer (1955) were opposed to Rogers' view. Father Marcel is of the view that, basically in principle and aim these two are not different, but in practice there are some differences. The psychotherapy and counselling could be visualized as being two ends of a continuum since psychotherapy deals with interpersonal problems, while counselling is on role definition problems. Vilmala defines counselling as a form of interviewing in which clients are helped to understand themselves more completely in order that they may correct an environmental or adjustment difficulty. The goal of counselling is to help the individual to clear away the entangling and hampering tentacles. The procedure for this is: guidance, clarification, suggestion, environmental manipulation, and use of common resources and its emphasis on conscious awareness, problem solving, education and supportive aspects. Pastoral counselling is also in line with the concepts of counselling mentioned above, which can also be called psychotherapy. One has to speak too about the person who undertakes the process of pastoral counselling.

III. TIPS FOR ENTERING PASTORAL COUNSELLING

The Pastoral Counsellor

No priest can avoid counselling unless he locks himself up in a room. Though he is not a psychologist he is called to do it. His duty of liberating people from bondage calls for this ministry too. In theological language a pastor is a prophet, priest and king. He is the minister of the Word, celebrant of the sacraments, and leader of the people. In all these priestly duties the major thrust is to lead the people of God. Through the sermon and Eucharist, he prepares to bring about transformation. His double-edged words cut their hearts to the quick, arouse consciousness and a call for a better life. The individual care of the people helps the process of transformation, and making whole. The American Association of Pastoral Counsellors defines a pastoral counsellor as "a minister who practises pastoral counselling at an advanced level which integrates religious resources and insights from the behavioural sciences."

The training of ministers is distinctive because it provides pastoral counsellors with a unique spiritual perspective on persons and their problems. Ministers are the only professionals who routinely have training in systematic theology, biblical studies, ethics and Church history. But a pastoral counsellor should have some training in psychology and counselling. However, pastoral counselling should not seek to mimic the counselling provided by the mental health professionals. "What ministers are uniquely equipped to do is to foster spiritual wholeness, and this should be the heart of any counselling that is called pastoral. This spiritual focus builds on the distinctive strengths of pastoral training and represents an approach to counselling that is not only consonant with other aspects of the pastoral role but also allows that counselling to be integrated within the context of pastoral care."

"Meier, Minirth and others place pastoral counsellors in the fifth and very important category. In most states they must work under the auspices of a church organization. While they are not licensed and most states do not have specific educational requirements for this designation, they should have a seminary degree in pastoral counselling. They also need to have a good undergraduate preparation in Bible and Theology, as well as Psychology and Counselling. The best seminary programme in pastoral counselling also meets the requirements for marriage and family counselling licensure, as pastors often need skills in this area." The Vatican council is well aware of the need of psychology and counselling today and suggests teaching them in the seminaries (OT 20).

The personality of the counsellor counts very much in this ministry. A mature and wholesome outlook on life is good for pastoral service. The more pastors are emotionally and psychologically mature, the better would they understand and accept this clients. In his models of counselling Carkhuff emphasizes the role of the counsellor: "clients of counsellors who offer high levels of facilitative and action-oriented conditions improve, while those of counsellors who offer low levels of these conditions, deteriorate."

Pastors are also unique in their social and symbolic role. People expect pastors to represent Christian values, beliefs, and commitments and to "bring Christian meaning to bear on human problems." The pastoral counsellor may function as an expert, an understanding helper, and a facilitator in the problem-solving process. Clinebell explains pastoral counselling in the context of the personality needs of a person. A person needs to love and to be loved; both can be spoken of as an authentic love experience in a dependable relationship. A pastoral counsellor helps people to handle their problems of living more adequately and of growing towards fulfilling their potentialities. This is achieved through reducing the inner blocks.

Today a common problem that creeps into the field of pastoral counselling, especially touching on the role of the pastoral counsellor is, that most of the pastoral counsellors are interested in giving a great deal of advice, which is a common failing. "While there are times when advice is needed, advice often goes unheeded, makes the person dependent on the counsellor and may hinder his growth as a Christian person."

Context and Goals of Pastoral Counselling

Pastoral counselling is done in the context of the Church. Hinter and Colston studied the process of counselling in different contexts and discovered that, there things being equal, counselling proceeded faster in a Church context (Hiltner and Colston 1961). They concluded that the reason for this was that the symbols and expectations associated with the Church made it clear right away where the pastoral counsellor stood on important value matters, thus lessening the period of time required by the person seeking help to get acquainted with the counsellor's values. Other common Church links such as a place of quiet or safety or a place where one meets God, also serve to facilitate the counselling within a Church context. The Church is a community of faith, a living congregation. A pastor could be a good problem solver in a united parish community, where he is accepted and welcomed. Another distinctive aspect of the context of pastoral counselling relates to the ongoing nature of contacts between pastor and parishioners. A pastor's counsel within a network of relationships where people know and see each other in a variety of situations enhances trust and thus greatly facilitates the counselling process.

The purpose of pastoral counselling is to facilitate spiritual growth. This involves helping people to understand their problems and their lives in the light of their relationship with God and as a consequence to live more fully in this relationship. Child (1990) suggests that pastoral counselling has two goals: to help parishioners help themselves and to help pastors develop a richer theological understanding of human nature. But while Benner feels that these outcomes may well be legitimate and even important by-products of pastoral counselling, the failure to recognize the primary goal of facilitating spiritual growth is a serious limitation of this or any other understanding of pastoral counselling. To suggest that pastoral counsellors have a primary concern for the facilitation of spiritual growth does not mean that they are concerned only, or even principally, with problems that appear to be spiritual. All problems have spiritual components because all of life is a blend of the religious or spiritual. So while pastoral counselling does not over look any area of a man's life, it does touch his physical, mental, social, cultural spheres and not merely the religious or spiritual. If pastoral counselling has to be done effectively to achieve its purpose, so has the time and place of its ministry to be contextualised.

Pastoral Counselling When, Where and How?

The pastor could counsel the person at his request, when a crisis or a problem suddenly occurs in his life, or as and when he so desires. Longer time counselling is required for long-term problems.

An hour should suffice for a counselling session. But a dozen or more members of the congregation should not monopolize the minister's time. Pastoral counselling needs privacy- a quiet room free from telephone, interruptions normally and time secured by an early appointment. The general approach to counselling should be friendly and business-like. Counselling is a pastoral activity that complements other activities. Hence if the candidate does not make progress, the pastor could use the preaching tool, or some other means of interaction as they present themselves. The counsellor should not thereby be burdened by his public duties as well as by pastoral counselling. The counsellor's aim is to help the client to detect the problem and so a Rogerian nondirective approach is a helpful beginning for the sessions.

There are various methods available for pastoral counselling which the pastoral counsellor deduces from his client's psychological and spiritual background, together with various resources contributing to this process.

Resources in Pastoral Counselling

Pastoral counselling is unique in its use of religious resources. Prayer, scripture, the sacraments, anointing with oil or the laying on of hands, and devotional or religious literature are all (depending on one's religious tradition) available as potential resources in the counselling process. The minister acts as a leader of a segment of the Christian community or fellowship... So in his total work, including counselling, he promotes Christian growth implicitly or explicitly. The pastor thus resolves not just a problem or situation but renders aid to a member of a fellowship; hence the person is assisted in growing in fellowship. Prayer sacraments, Scripture reading or doctrinal discussions function as religious elements in counselling and help substantially in cementing closer fellowships. Kay and Weaver say, " the Christian minister in on much safer theological grounds in emphasizing the reality of a new birth, the operation of the Holy Spirit in enabling the individual to overcome sin and the power of persistent prayer." We should take note, however, that these religious resources are evident first and foremost in the pastoral counsellor's own life. If they are being used significantly in the personal life of the pastor can they not be employed appropriately in counselling?

The pastor's awareness of both the person's problems as well as his or her present attitudes and religious background must necessarily precede the appropriate use of religious resources in counselling. Besides, before using such resources the pastor should have the conviction that they are meaningful and hence will evoke appreciation and a ready response. This respect for the person's feelings and beliefs will often open up a healthy lively discussion on spiritual conflicts and blocks. On the other hand, even if the person shows a dislike for prayer or scripture in the session, this in no way limits using prayer at other times. Clinebell notes that religious resources should be used in ways that empower the person, rather than in ways that might diminish his or her sense of initiative, strength, or responsibility.

The essence of these religious resources is the dynamic contact they can provide between God and the one seeking pastoral help. Their use must never, therefore, be mechanical, legalistic, or magical. If used sensitively, they can uniquely help the person sense the caring, healing, and sustaining presence of a personal God. Today's pastoral counselling uses all these resources in a broader sense. This leads us to the nature of pastoral counselling in our day.

Pastoral Counselling Today

A formal pastoral counselling is an emerging need of the Kerala Church. The dissociated, frustrated individual in the parish context is a great threat for development. Besides alcohol, drugs, superstitious beliefs, lack of education and poor faith aggravate the situation.

In the U.S.A studies report that pastoral counselling consumes 6-20% of a clergyman's time or 2.5-12 hours per week. "The most frequently cited counselling issues include marital and family problems, feelings of depression, guilt, anxiety and stress, and religious and spiritual concerns," while sexual and suicidal issues are less common. The US clergy are mainly engaged in formal pastoral counselling. Pastoral counselling is considered as " a type of pastoral care, structured and focused on a specially articulated need, or concern involving some degree of 'contract' in which a request for help is articulated...." N.S.Wood draws attention to the women practitioners' struggle in identifying issues in pastoral counselling, from a Protestantine perspective; and since it pertains less frequently to women, it is not the focus of our study. John L. Maes asks "Can Pastoral Counselling flourish is a World of Managed Care?" and he throws much light on certain possibilities, emphasizing short term therapy, family therapy, utilizing in-house interviews and interview and review techniques, and developing and maintaining strong relationships with other health care professionals.

Advantages and Limitations of Pastoral Counselling

Pastoral counselling is related to other forms of counselling, but it is also distinctively different from other forms if any. The major advantages are: minister's training in Theology, the discernment of the spiritual, the use of religious resources, the facilitation and thrust and the acceleration of the counselling processes as a representative of the Church. The opportunities to use the resources of congregational life, and to take initiatives in establishing a counselling relationship and the possibility of early intervention, besides the availability of the counselling services regardless of the ability to pay are advantageous.

We can't glibly pass by the limitations we face in the process of pastoral counselling. Some of them are: the limitation of time due to other pressing responsibilities; training of the pastors especially in psychology, the pastor's dislikes and conflicts with those who are seen in various other roles; free services, etc...

IV. DIFFERENT OCCASIONS

There is a growing tendency among people to turn to their pastors seeking the opportunity with the help of his expertise to look at themselves and their problems, in just this perspective, namely in the light of faith and religious traditions. A pastor is not free from any of the vicissitudes of a person's life, since his ministry is not a time bound duty but forever. From birth to death the pastor plays an important role. The sacraments touch the entire life of the person through baptism, confirmation, Eucharist, reconciliation, anointing of the sick, marriage, and priesthood. In all these the priest gives new life to a person as a Christian, immerses and anoints with oil, feeds him, consoles him and forgives his wrong doings, heals his wounds, and helps him to select a role in life forever. Pastoral counselling attends to all these functions, be it in infancy, childhood, or adulthood. Pastoral counselling extends its service to all who avail themselves of it regardless of their qualifications, gender or class distinction. A pastor may have to counsel an individual, or an entire family, or group.

Some of the more common issues that call for pastoral counselling are: a) marriage and family relationships, b) sickness and healing, c) depression, low self-esteem, d) death and bereavement. Some are still more important issues are of suicide, alcoholism, drug addiction, and chronic ill health issues.

Marriage, Family Relations and Growth

Marriage is the blissful union that promotes for procreation and fructifies the earth. Unfortunately modernization and its various consequences oppress the family, creating many hard core problems within the family itself and society in general. The increased number of divorces, and broken families, point to the relevance and the indispensability of counselling.

According to Fr. Manalel, "in married life two basic types of problems may arise:

1) Those involving the individual personality and adjustment of the married partners, and

2) those related more to marriage itself." There are diverse far-reaching character problems that seriously aggravate married life. Some of them are *financial issues* especially the dowry problems; differences in the *social life* of the partners; *parent-child relationships; job pressures* imposed on marriage; *sexual conflicts* like impotency, sexual diseases, premarital sex issues; concepts of the *roles played by husband and wife*; the need to dominate on the part of one or both the mates because of status, education, etc.; and *in-law problems* especially with the mother-in-law and sisters-in-law. There are also some other problems like alcoholism, gambling, extreme jealousy, compulsive nagging, chronic complaining, excessive suspicion and possessiveness, uncontrollable children, depression and disorders/sickly children, elderly parents and violent temper. Divorce is fast becoming a common feature in the Kerala society. "The outcome of divorce almost always results in a distressed life. Still, divorce may be the only alternative to living in a distressed marriage."

Counselling the family has its roots in the growth and development of both child guidance and professional marriage counselling. Family therapy is a form of psychotherapy that deals with interpersonal issues and involves in-person contacts with members of a family. Often it is a particular concern about the problems of one family member identified as the 'patient,' than cognition of the need of help for the family as a whole.

Some of the theoretical concepts for family therapy are the *family as a system*, which means that the members of a family interact with each other in interlocking patterns; *circularity*, family problems occurring within the context of circular interlocking loops in their collective relationships that become repetitive over time; and *triangles*, means instead of dealing with the problems between the two of them, they spend much time and energy on the child.

There are a number of models of family therapy that have developed over a period of time, with similarities and differences in practice. Some of them are: *Object relations-integration model* (Famo, 1981; Bosozormenyi-Nagy, 1973 and Paul, 1980), *Bowen model* (1978), the *Structural model* (Minuchin, 1974; Minuchin & Fishman, 1981), the *Experiential model* (Napier & Whitaker,1978; Kempler, 1981), the *Communication model* (Bateson,1956; Madanes, 1984) and *Psycho education model* (Falloon, Boyd & McGill, 1984).

The goals in counselling marriage occasions, are to resolve interpersonal conflicts, to encourage each individual to meet the emotional needs of the mate, to clarify role relations and to strengthen the ability of each to cope in a healthy manner with stress in marriage. The supportive and non-directive form of counselling appropriate to individuals is less effective with the family. Instead, the counsellor acts more as a mediator and facilitator in trying to persuade the family to follow a common aim. When a couple comes in for marriage counselling, establish what their objectives are in the first session and make it clear that each spouse has to try to change him/herself, and not the other. The counsellor's strategy is to propose a family plan and monitor it.

A pastor could also help by including some general teaching on a subject in his sermons; by organizing adult and youth group meetings and seminars from time to time to discuss particular problems and questions; by giving 'premarital' counselling to prepare engaged couples or those about to get engaged for their future life together; by making sure that every wedding service he conducts, reflects the true meaning of Christian marriage, so that all those who participate, clearly understand what they are doing, and by encouraging people who are experiencing problems in their marriage to come to him for counselling. He should help couples to grow in Christ and in His love, encourage them to pray and dine together.

The family is the blissful set up that contains various age groups and this in a dynamic growth. Adolescence is considered as a crucial period because of the emotional, psychological and physiological changes taking place in one's life. Formal counsellors are viewed by adolescents as people who will tell them they are not okay. Teachers, neighbours, youth coordinators are the people to whom the adolescents turn to as a first line of defence against the crisis they face as part of growing up. From the twenty years experience of James Archer with college students he says suicide and depression are the most difficult kinds of student problems every one handles.

Working with adolescents requires doing some thing practical for them; this can be a positive starting point in gaining trust. They need concrete assistance in settling the disputes between themselves. Familiarity with the client's family only tends to aggravate these disputes. Since they are action oriented, they can become quickly disillusioned when the sessions do not immediately relieve their distress.

There is no magical line that separates adolescence, from adulthood, yet it is considered to be the age of twenty. As a young adult a person has to seek an employment, attend to other emerging needs such as friendship, sexuality, intimate relationship and other problems like managing a home, parenting, separation/ divorce.

A person, who has reached the age of about 40, whose children are approaching adulthood and whose parents are ageing and dying, face a crucial period in mid life. Development in mid-life can be characterized by Erickson's psychosocial stage of *generativity versus stagnation*. The inability to handle the challenges of mid-life may precipitate mid-life crisis, which manifests itself in depression, marital problems, excessive uncertainty, and feelings of futility. Here one has to face the problems of career goals, find time for leisure, and resolve some other issues of parenting and of ageing parents. The middle-aged adults are found to be distressed due to anticipation of loss, regrets regarding an unsatisfactory relationship, burdens related to care giving, and awareness of their own morality. The family, marriage and the growth and development of a person especially in the period of his/ her adolescence and adulthood are the real situations a pastor has to deal with other than sickness and healing.

Sickness and Healing

Suffering and sickness are the problems that man has long tried to answer and still they remain unresolved and unanswered. Nothing concerns the sick person expect his illness and the restoration to health. Most of the seriously ill people wonder why life is so burdensome. Often they religiously associate and attribute it to their sinful past. Guilt feeling and moral gravity are the net result of this. "The pastoral counsellor would do well to combat this guilty reaction with an attitude of compassion."

Therefore to help people effectively in time of healing and suffering, a pastor needs to know: the cultural ideas of the person or the people concerned; the Church's ideas about sickness, the role of the medical workers in the area and the social and economic situation of the sick person's family and other dependents, who may need practical help in carrying on their daily routine. Besides the above mentioned background factors the pastor must know the psychological dimensions of the sick person. One writer distinguishes between a disease and injury as 'something which happens to a person's physical body'; and an illness as 'an experience involving the person's feelings and attitudes towards the disease and towards other people.' Some of the feelings most people usually experience as a result of falling sick are: *fear* of pain and suffering, *anxiety* about the possible causes and results of sickness, *isolation and rejection* from the family and friends especially when they are hospitalised for a long time, *uselessness* experienced by the busy and skilled people, *anger* towards those who are well or toward the doctor, *hopelessness* when the sickness is prolonged and *escapism* by avoiding responsibility or escaping from an unpleasant situation.

The goal of pastoral counselling is the total health of the human person. According to Benedict M. Ashley, persons who are ill faced with potentially serious problems, fear of suffering and death, the tedium of a long boring stay in the hospital; uncertainties of diagnosis and prognosis and fear of various tests and treatment procedures; separation from regular work; worry and perhaps guilt feeling regarding the various responsibilities at home, also suffer a sense of deprivation of privacy and freedom and are unable to accept what has happened to them.

In this case besides providing care for the above-mentioned areas the pastor could pray with the patient. The sacraments of the Eucharist, anointing of the sick and reconciliation could be meaningfully administered bringing the much needed comfort and sense of security.

Health counselling is another field which on some occasions at least the pastoral counsellor has to deal with. Health counselling is a discipline growing in the field of health psychology, which attempts the promotion of health, the preservation and treatment of illness. Health counsellors intervene at four levels: biological, affective, cognitive and behavioural. Problem areas such as stress disorders, appetite disorders, infertility, premenstrual syndrome, menopause, pregnancy, and AIDS have been studied and been addressed by them. In the pastoral setting too the pastor has to face many of these problems. Besides these the pastor may have chances during counselling to comfort people with communication disorder and vision impairment.

The stress related disorders like heart disease, hypertension, cancer, headaches, obesity, eating disorders, smoking, etc. are also some major concerns of the pastor. The role of the counsellor is not to make decisions for the clients, but to help them to take decisions themselves. Stress reduction procedures particularly relaxation training, imagery, and biofeedback could be suggested. Decreased public tolerance for smoking and legislation against smoking contribute to the prevention of smoking. Providing them appropriate information and solid decision-making skills could help them. They should help the clients to clarify their values e.g., moral and religious issues in case of infertility, abortion, etc. HIV patients are problematic. Their unresolved personal grief, and the inspiration afforded by the patients' heroic struggle with the illness and their mortality prompts us to offer supportive care that could empower them to persist in their struggle. Pastors too can help the family members through their feelings about the illness, and if the disease is terminal, to help them confront death in a more courageous way.

The pastor has chances to intervene in the problems of people with obsessive-compulsive, phobic and personality disorders. Behaviour therapy and pharmacological treatment is usually used in OCD while the pastor may help them by instructing the families to accept the patients despite the doubtfulness of the disease. Support groups both to the family and patients are helpful.

Alcohol is a social evil, against which there is much protest. The Church is also very active in this field. The realization of our society is that the cause of a great number of family problems, crimes and anti-social behaviour is due to this alcohol dependency. A priest can casually counsel one who is addicted. Alcohol dependence is the physical component of the disease that has come to be known as alcoholism. Rosette defines it as a *three- headed dragon,* of which the first head is physical dependence and the other two heads represent the psychological and spiritual components of the disease.

The Oxford Movement was a spiritual fellowship that sought to recapture the values of early Christianity through a programme of personal self-development and caused the rise of Alcoholics Anonymous (AA) 1935-39. The fellowship established a blue print for developing spiritual maturity, contained in 12 Steps, and a group code of ethics, the 12 Traditions. Another problem a pastor has to deal with at least in some cases is loss of meaning in one's life due to failure in attempted chances on one's life.

Depression and Low Self-Esteem

It is very difficult for those who do not feel depression to understand those who are immersed in it. Depression is something altogether more deep-seated than a flattening of the emotions or a sense of deep sadness. It appears to grip the will and hinder the ability to think. Consequently, depression affects not only the feelings but also ones behaviour. Sleeplessness, lack of concentration, finding no pleasure in relationship, loss of appetite is some of the symptoms that accompany it.

Certain tendencies in depression are triggered by external events. The breakup of relationships, loss of a loved one, unattained aspirations, loss of a job, financial crisis all these can well be factors for the defective personality to suffer from depression. The supportive and non-directive form of counselling appropriate to individuals is less effective with a family. Instead the counsellor acts more as a mediator and facilitator in trying to persuade the family to follow a common aim. The counsellor will do well to bear in mind that families function best when each person has a job or a role that does not conflict with that of the others but which contributes to the good of all.

Low self-esteem often accompanies depression. The depressed persons feel that they are not adequately loved and being indecisive they constantly need approval. In an attempt to compensate for low self-esteem, it is common for people to speak disparagingly about others. The counsellor is able to provide non-judgmental warmth that will counteract many of the causes of low self-esteem. Low self-esteem is a state of mind that has emotional consequences and, once the state of mind changes, the emotion gradually follows. The good news of Jesus is a great remedy against low self-esteem.

Death and Bereavement

Death is another situation that a pastor has to face in his ministry. What should be done to the bereaved person is a real question the pastor is baffled with. The minister may feel there is nothing to be said apart from assuring the bereaved that he or she is not to blame. In fact bereaved people often feel like social outcasts because they know that whenever they walk into a room or meet friends they feel like wet blankets. The priest may help the relatives of the dead person by helping them to conduct the funeral and the anniversaries in a suitable manner. If church members expect the visit of the pastor immediately after a death occurs, so too do the nominal Christians. By lending a listening ear the pastor can encourage people to express their deepest feelings. Usually after the first weeks of death the relatives and friends will be there to console the family members, but after that a pastor's visit will help them to tide over the feeling of shock, even depression, of being uncared for and abandoned. If visits are not possible the pastor could write letters of condolence or ask the neighbouring Christians to visit the family.

Counselling in Religious Issues

There are some who are really confronted with religious content or connotations. Religion has special perspectives and issues, some of which are: abortion, alcoholism, homosexuality, pleasure and sex, sin, etc... which are prohibited by Christian standards and concepts of morality. While there are some other issues like death-grief and mourning, depression, devil-Satan and angels, the Holy Spirit, love-marriages and divorce, women and men etc... The new religious movement like the Charismatic Movement underscores sin and focuses on praise. The *Gethsemane Prayer Groups* conduct vigil services, but the prayer *gatherings* and money motivated prayer gangs often lead people to abnormality.

The pastoral counsellor has opportunities to explain why there is illness and pain in the life of the innocent and blameless and to console them through the eyes of faith. In the case of abortion, the counsellor must be clear about his values while recognizing that to offer or assert these values may leave the client with consequences the counsellor does not have to shoulder. As the Bible too has set its limits on the use of alcohol, the client who wishes to give up the habit of drink must be helped by the parish church through prohibition of alcohol. The malignant figure of Satan can permit the client to evade responsibility for his behaviour. The true knowledge of the Holy Spirit is very necessary today, because of pathological experiences. The Bible too forbids homosexual acts. Certain clients furnish a detailed list of specific sins. "Such lists are inconsistent with Jesus, who is more concerned about attitudes than behavioural trivia, with alienation from God than empty ritual. Trying to open up such feelings is initially painful, but if the counsellor does so in a manner that expresses interest in the client's feelings without endorsing their accuracy, then a healing process can be initiated."

In dealing with religious issues Lovinger reiterates, that "the client's need for total trust right at the start of the counselling, suggests fragility, an absurd history or great difficulty with ambiguity. Accepting assurance without qualm connotes considerable desperation. The wish to be identical with the counsellor shows a poorly organized self. To present a direct question, and offer information without understanding its meaning may burden a client with unnecessary knowledge." In contrast to the vast field of today's pastoral counsellors Dobson suggests a pattern of referral, which merely reduces the cases to be referred to as "encountering problems that are both psychological and spiritual (may also need one of the other sources listed above), and if qualified they may also deal with marital conflicts, divorce, childrearing problems, etc...

ICD-10 classification of mental and behavioural disorders gives a set of disorders that are mostly found in pastoral counselling. They generally fall in the category F and Z viz., The unspecified mental disorder (F99), factors influencing health status and contact with health services (Z00-99).Under the category Z one could highlight some of them as: care involving use of rehabilitation Z-50, problems related to education and literacy Z-55, problems related to unemployment Z-56, problems related to housing and economic circumstances Z59, problems related to social environment, problems related to negative life events in childhood Z- 61, other problems related to upbringing eg. Over protection, institutional upbringing Z-62, primary support group including family circumstances Z-63, psycho social circumstances Z-64&65, counselling related to sexual behaviour Z-70, life style Z-72, life management difficulty Z-73 etc...

V. VARIOUS APPROACHES IN COUNSELLING

Pastoral counselling received its methods of counselling, having roots in different secular psychologies. Pastoral counselling uses different methods ranging from the long period directive methods to short duration brief therapy, non-directive and solution focused approaches. In recent years, pastoral counselling has become a massive complex subject where a variety of systems and approaches are advocated. It has been estimated that there are over 400 different approaches to counselling currently in use. While counselling itself is seeking to reach an agreement about its methods and parameters, the relationship between pastoral theology and counselling is bound to remain fluid. The different approaches used in pastoral counselling are outlined as follows.

1. Psychodynamic Approaches

Psychoanalysis

The classical Freudian theory that investigates a person's inner life, assumes that the individual is the sum of his/her instincts. Freud's experience with his patients led him to the conclusion that the source of "neurosis" was anxiety experienced by the ego when unacceptable unconscious drives threatened to break through into the conscious mind. In order to deal with this threat the ego had recourse to a number of defense mechanisms, the most important of which was repression. However while the impulse could be buried the effort involved, weakened the ego considerably. Furthermore, some anxiety remained, forcing its victims into various self-defeating postures and generally making them miserable. Thus according to Freud, the proper treatment for neurosis was to coax the unconscious impulse out into consciousness so that the patient could at least confront it. Once confronted and 'worked through' this material would lose its power to terrorize the ego. Self-defeating defences could accordingly be abandoned, and the ego would then be free to devote itself to more constructive pursuits. As Freud succinctly put it, "where id was, there shall ego be"

To treat anxiety disorders Freud found this method, in which people can be helped only when they recognize and deal with their repressed feelings. Hence the aim of the therapy is to help people identify their 'hidden emotions', bring them into the open and deal with them. Freud made use of hypnosis in his early years of practice, but later dropped it in favour of free association. For this he mainly relied on the techniques of free association and dream analysis. This time consuming 'talking cure' seems to be non- directive although the analyst is undoubtedly a powerful and influential figure'. The Christian method of "memory healing" or "inner healing" generally shares with psychoanalysis as emphasis upon healing at the depths of one's being. Clients are encouraged to relax and are then asked to describe early problem experiences. As clients attempt to relive those experiences, the counsellor encourages them to ask God to forgive those who wronged them. God is then asked to erase the pain of the memory; the client may imagine Christ helping in the situation. Freud's views have been variously altered by subsequent analysis. Alfred Adler stressed aggression and the will to power. Carl Jung openly acknowledged the supernatural in human psychology and Otto Rank argued that the trauma of birth is the origin of neurosis. Neo- Freudians, such as Karen Horney and Erich Fromm see people as social beings and aim to help achieve inner strength and improved relationships, adopting more 'here and now' and the directive techniques. Freud's daughter Anna Freud amplified his ideas and theories on having a great importance for the ego and defence mechanisms. Melanie Klein and her followers modified them, developing 'Object–Relations' theory and its emphasis on the first year of one's life.

Object Relations Theory

Melanie Klein (1892- 1960) was strongly influenced by Sigmund Freud and Karl Abraham. She moved beyond Freudian emphasis on biological instincts to stress the significance of object relations, i.e. the emotional components of a child's relationships with his or her social environment.

Klein argued that the patterns of the emotional response learned in childhood are repeated later in life. The child typically develops from a stage of omnipotence into the paranoid- schizoid positions, in which the external world is perceived to be split into part objects, some nourishing, others threatening. At this stage persecutory anxieties can arise. Normal development in a good environment enables the child to grow into the depressive position, in which the world can be perceived as the ambiguous whole objects, and in which feelings of guilt arise. A satisfactory growth through this stage enables the child to learn to express creativity and concern.

2. Behavioural Approach

This method uses the ideas of J.B. Watson, B.F. Skinner and his followers like Hans Eysenck and Joseph Wolpe. In this approach the inner thoughts and feelings of the client are ignored in favour of a concentration on behaviour. The fundamental principle is that most behaviour, both normal and abnormal, is learned, from the external stimuli rather than from the inner world of thoughts and feelings.

Hence to change behaviour, an insight into the foundations of one's personality is not sufficient. If the behaviour is to be changed, it must be attacked directly, using the same mechanism of learning that created the behaviour in the first place. The attempts to change behaviour are made by acts of rewards and punishments and the main concern of the behaviourist counsellor is not to interpret the client's behaviour but to modify it.

A maladaptive behaviour is maintained not by past conditions but by current conditions, which may be different from the circumstances that originally produced the behaviour. So treatment emphasizes the stimuli that elicit and reinforce the problem behaviour in the present.

The therapeutic manner is more pragmatic. Behaviourists define maladaptive behaviour in terms of three components: behavioural, emotional and cognitive. The primary goal is a change in the overt behaviour, the treatment usually operant conditioning when the primary goal is a change in emotion; the treatment generally centers on respondent conditioning, and when the goal is changing cognition the therapist uses the techniques of cognitive restructuring.

The behavioural approach has been turned to good use in therapy through relaxation techniques, the desensitization, modelling, implosive therapy, flooding, so that the feared task can be achieved. Training in assertiveness, aversion therapy and token economy are some other methods of treatment.. Attempts to change the behaviour often lead to directive styles of counselling. A number of methodologies utilize cognitive as well as behavioural approaches, for e.g. Glassers' reality therapy and Ellis' Rational Emotive Therapy.

Reality Therapy   Dr. William Glasser's *Reality Therapy* was published in New York in 1965. Glasser rejected the concept of mental illness that "people do not act irresponsibly because they are ill, rather they are ill because they act irresponsibly. The mental ills are unable to satisfy their basic needs of relatedness and respect in a responsible way, because they deny the reality of their world.

According to Glasser the human need to love and to be loved and to feel that we are worthwhile to ourselves and to others, are bound up with maintaining a certain standard of behaviour. Morals, standards and values are all intimately related to the fulfilment of our need for self-esteem. The acquiring of responsibility thus becomes an essential ingredient for reality therapy, and this can be achieved through developing an emotional relationship between the client and therapist. Facilitating a sense of responsibility is the skill of this therapy.

Rational Emotive Therapy (RET)

Albert Ellis' RET (Ellis and Grieger, 1977) has its core postulate in the stoic philosopher Epictetus' phrase "men are disturbed not by things but by views which they take of them". RET is active and directive. Ellis believes that our problems are not the result of how we feel, rather he suggests how we think and believe determines how well we will adjust to our environment. RET is taught in an A-B-C format. People often assume that Activating events (A) cause them to experience certain emotional consequences (C) e.g. 'My wife left me so I feel awful'. But activating events have consequences only through the mediation of our Beliefs (B) about those events. Thus a rational belief results in a rational consequence and an irrational, belief in an irrational consequence.

The goal of therapy is to minimise a self-defeating outlook and help an individual acquire a more realistic, total philosophy of life. Counselling in the RET system consists of education; understanding the irrational beliefs that are producing irrational beliefs that cause subjective distress in a person and assisting him to change these irrational beliefs. Thus restructuring the way people think and believe is the remedy. RET focuses on the present, and while irrational beliefs may have been learned in the past, the problem is in the present. RET says that enjoyment and survival are the main goals in life and implies that individuals are not bound by the moral commandments found in most of the world 'religions'.

3. Humanistic and Existential.

Carl Rogers and Abraham Maslow are well-known advocates of a humanistic psychology, which reflects Wilhelm Dilthey's emphasis on personal integration, besides insisting that people have all the resources needed for change. These approaches share the common objective

of helping the patients to become more truly "themselves"-
to seek meaning from life and then to make deliberate
choices in order to live more meaningfully. Roger's non-
directiveness and client centeredness, avowedly a reaction
to Behaviourism and Freudianism, have greatly influenced
the rise of the Counselling movements of the 1940s and
1950s.

Client Centred Therapy

The best known and popular humanist therapy is Carl
Roger's Client centred therapy (1951). Rogerian
counselling was central to the pastoral counselling
movement in its formative period. Roger holds the view
that people are "innately motivated to actualise their
potential. The only way to solve the problem of poor
adjustment and unhappiness is to eliminate unrealistic
conditions. The means to this end is client-centred therapy.
This focuses directly on the client's individual personality,
not on any system of theories or laws regarding human
behaviour in general. In the effort to reconcile the clients
to their true selves, the therapist attempts to see the world
through their eyes, so that they come to regard their own
experience of the world as a thing of value. The therapists'
ability to do this depends on three basic factors: namely
(1) the *unconditional positive regard*-a total acceptance
hoping by this means to induce the clients to accept the
totality of their experience. (2) *empathetic understanding*-
means hearing that resonates on all possible levels to what
they are communicating, (3) *"realness"*- that is the ability
to realize and verbalize what they are experiencing at a
given time. "The Jesus Model" of MC Kenna (1977),
includes many components of client-centered therapy. For

e.g., he explains Christ's encounter with the Samaritan woman (John 4,1-42) using many of the concepts of the Rogerian approach, although he notes other psychological and spiritual dynamics as well.

Existential psychology has been influenced by the philosophy of Sore Kierkegaard, which later contributed to the thinking of Viktor Frankl, whose logo therapy stresses meaning and spiritual core in human life.

Logo Therapy

Viktor Frankl the Father of logo therapy (*Man's Search for Meaning, 1959*), was a psychiatrist and a long-term prisoner in inhuman Nazi concentration camps, which found him deprived of everything except a bare existence. 'Logos' is a Greek word, which denotes "meaning". Logo therapy aims at healing a man by helping him find the meaning, the purpose of his life and to make him commit himself to its realization. Man's 'will-to- meaning' is frustrated and is termed 'existential frustration.' Frankl distinguishes several types of neurosis, and traces some of them (noogenic neurosis) to the failure of the sufferer to find meaning and a sense of responsibility in his existence. Freud stresses frustration in the sexual life. Frankl`s, frustration is the "will to meaning". The meaning of life may be found in three ways: by doing something, by experiencing a value in the meaning of suffering. "As a technique, logo therapy is to replace anticipatory anxiety by paradoxical intention, hyper-intention and hyper-reflection by dereliction. And dereliction is only by reorienting life toward a client's specific vocation and mission in life". Many today search for meaning, meaning that only God can give. As Augustine states, there is a

God-shaped vacuum that only God can fill. People continue to search until they find God or some substitute. Realizing the fact of that search and the need for an adequate answer for the meaning to life can be an important aspect of pastoral counselling, and Christ aids the solution to man's search for meaning.

4. Spiritual/Transpersonal

A great number of existentialists and humanistic thinkers discontent with human nature's inability to set its own house in order have turned to spiritual or transpersonal approaches. Here fulfilment is sought beyond the personal realms, in the higher self, unity consciousness, the cosmos or God. Forms of meditation, deep-breathing exercises, yoga etc aid this search... Some other areas in this perspective include Roberto Assagioli's psychosynthesis, using techniques of imaginative journeying, music therapy and Jungian views.

Psychosynthesis

It is an approach developed by Roberto Assagioli, as a process of personal growth. In a more specific sense it is a conscious attempt to cooperate with the natural processes of personal development. Psychosynthesis utilizes many techniques of psychological action, aiming first at the development and perfection of the personality, and then at its harmonious coordination and increasing unification with the self; these phases may be called respectively 'personal' and 'spiritual' psychosynthesis. Thus it becomes a psychological development treatment method and integral education.

Assagioli uses the 'egg-diagram' that represents our total psyche, and the 'star-diagram' representing our psychological functions to explain his theory. "Psychosynthesis is the formation or reconstruction of the personality around the unifying centre which includes the following stages: through knowledge of one's personality, control of its various elements, realization of one's true self- the discovery or creation of the unifying centre and finally psychosynthesis: the formation of personality around new centre." There is a sub-personality in a person and it is a synthesis of habit patterns, traits, complexes and other psychological elements. But in order to have a synthesis, there has to be a centre around which the synthesis occurs; the "I" is the personal centre of identity.

Psychosynthesis is not only a method for self-realization, but also a continuous and organic process that is happening in the psyche of everyone at all times. The methods used for personal psychosynthesis are many: such as catharsis, critical analysis, self-identification, dis-identification, use of the imagination, visualization etc...

Nouthetic Counselling

It is based on the Greek term for warning, exhortation, and admonition i.e. "nouthetic" Jay Adams presented this approach as a series of organized and regular sessions between the pastor and the person. After diagnosing the problem, the pastor helps in a person-to-person verbal confrontation to bring about change in the behaviour and attitudes of the counselee; for this the source is the Bible. This approach is authentic, directive and more disciplining through which the counselee actively tries out new habits. Adams opines that dehabitation and rehabitation occur together and as bad habits die out, good habits replace them. The whole process can take place in about twelve weeks. This approach is more cognitive and behavioural than emotional. The methods to promote this process may include rewards and punishments but not cruel ones. Adams' approach is controversial because it is against Rogerian and Freudian currents and it is unwise to attribute all stresses and emotional problems to personal sins and irresponsibility (Meier) and deny the existence of mental illness (Hurding).

5. Mixed Approaches

It is true to say that the above mentioned approaches in various mixtures have contributed to the so called newer therapies such as Gestalt, Psycho-drama, primal therapy, cognitive therapy, TA, Neuro-linguistic programming and co-counselling. For a general understanding some of these theories are explained below.

Gestalt Therapy

Frederick S. Perls a proponent of the therapy (1969), was influenced by K. Lewin, Werthimer and Kohler. "He says that their most important idea was that of unfinished situation, the incomplete gestalt, and makes this a major concept in this theory- the differentiation of the Gestalt into the figure and ground". Gestalt therapy was concerned about how clients perceive their own feelings emotions and bodily sensations.

In a healthy person, figure and ground are sharply differentiated, not confused. Therefore in a healthy person, behaviour is selective. The Gestalt formation and destruction is a continuous process. It can be interfered with in three ways;

a. By poor perceptual contact with the external world and body.

b. By blocking the open expression of needs, or

c. By repression or "holding back' of a muscular response to the need.

Awareness is the hub of the Gestalt therapy approach. The awareness of needs and how they are blocked are the particular insights of Perls' theory. Using various techniques self-awareness and responsibility are increased. Role playing and empty chair techniques are some means for the praxis of this theory.

Transactional Analysis

Eric Berne defines TA as "a theory of personality and social action, and a clinical method of psychotherapy, based on the analysis of all possible transactions between two or more people, on the basis of specifically defined ego states". The major TA concept is that people can be autonomous. The TA theory can be summarized as:

a. Structural Analysis- segregations and analysis of parent, child and adult ego states which comprise individual personality.

b. TA proper- determining which ego state in one person is transacting with which ego state in another and in what ways.

c. Game analysis- analysis of a series of overt social transactions, which by convert ulterior transactions, lead to a well defined payout.

d. Script analysis- analysis of life dramas that people, usually without awareness, act out compulsively.

In TA participants are encouraged to analyse their transactions with one another and to disrupt them by refusing to act according to the time hour rules. Basic conflicts may then come to the surface, where they can be discussed openly. The goal is to show people that their interpersonal coping patterns, no matter how natural they feel, may be very destructive and to give them a chance to try out new ways of relating to others.

The interest of knowing the human mind and behaviour led to the finding of wide varieties of approaches in counselling and psychotherapy. There are many other approaches to the above-mentioned streams of psychology. Pastoral counselling has not yet developed as an independent branch until today. It uses a large variety of approaches according to the interest of the counsellor.

The literature on pastoral counselling is divided regarding the possibility of reconciling secular and pastoral theories. Some pastoral counsellors would disavow almost all, if not all secular theories simply because they believe that any theory without a religious foundation cannot deal effectively with solutions to problems in the world. Some pastoral counsellors would agree with secular theories that reflect an approach compatible with the theological understanding of human beings and the work of God. Still others accept any and all advances in the psychological field without any critical examination of the theory or its underlying principles. Much of pastoral counselling literature deals with issues inevitably raised by any radical interdisciplinary and radically systemic approach to viewing the whole human condition (physical, psychological, social, ethical, and spiritual). Though the authors of pastoral counselling vary in their view, one could never avoid the aspect of religious dimension; of God as the third party in the process of pastoral counselling, which makes it pastoral, through the church paradigm. An analysis of various counselling methods and approaches is essential to find possible and suitable methods required for pastoral counselling in its *sitz im leben* of the church.

VI. APPLICATION OF VARIOUS COUNSELLING METHODS

There are many approaches used in pastoral counselling pertaining to the various psychological theories. One could apply any method in the process of pastoral counselling. Though various approaches have been mentioned in the last chapter, here the focus is on the proper method of pastoral counselling. Different schools approach pastoral counselling differently hence there are a good number of methods to be discussed, from different angles of person, group and family. The first part of this chapter is an analysis of the literature on the various methods of counselling, while the second is on a methodology of study.

Various Particular Methods of Pastoral Counselling

G. Brake in his ministry of pastoral counselling in Panama says, "The counsellors' primary task is to deal with the person's actual condition as he or she experiences it. I tread softly before those I care for in pastoral counselling. I never want to rush in and solve a problem. I desire to treat others as I would want to be treated."

D. Gastonguay also agrees on the process of pastoral counselling as, that which unfolds precisely within and through the relationship between the client and the counsellor. His process involves *teaming-up, taming, you and me becoming us* and *toward termination*. The universal counsellor is nonexistent, and both counsellor and client will have to feel the inner invitation to move into something more personal.

A person comes for help, when he deviates from the normal stream of life. The psychoanalytic perspective on such an individual is an opening for the further exposition of different methods on pastoral counselling.

The dimensions of emotional disturbances vary, being either psychosis, neurosis, disorders of personality and character structure etc... or both object relatedness, which means that the ability of a person to interact meaningfully and realistically with others , can be distorted. Narcissism and the experience of the self can be explained as follows: the experience of, and relationship with he or she includes the capacity to maintain an integrated sense of itself; an adequate level of self- esteem, and a set of sound, consistent and realistic values. Disturbances in self-esteem are reflected in a variety of symptoms, such as a sense of emptiness, a selfish use of others, and problems in empathy, work inhibitions, and perverse sexual activities. Other narcissistic disorders involve a subjective sense of impairment with respect to self definition, self-concept, self-worth, self-esteem and self continuity, as well as the highly selfish use of others as a means of gratifying needs for aggrandizement, self-value reassurance and the like.

Symptoms of acute and chronic emotional disorders include disturbances in effect as anxiety, depression, boredom, and anger and specific symptom complexes such as obsessive and/ or compulsive symptoms, inhibitions, phobias, and hysterical symptoms; these may be acute or chronic, the latter seen as suspiciousness, hypochondriasis, chronic anxiety, etc...

Emotional disturbances are dysfunctions within the individual that are based on some type of psychological disturbances. They are derived from two interrelated sources, 1. maternal (environmental failures and other external pathological influences) and 2. intra psychic malfunctions and unresolved conflicts. Emotional disturbances are based on and expressed through an unconscious process and fantasy-projections. They are founded largely upon an unconscious communicative process and their maintenance relies on effects taking place outside of the awareness of the individual. Emotional disturbances having complex structures include disturbances in the area of object relatedness, narcissism, psychic structure and communication. Neurosis formation tends to impair the relative autonomy of the individual, to cause psychic pain and to interfere with maturation, growth and development and individuation.

Thus a person who is emotionally disturbed is alienated from himself, others and from the Ultimate, God. The methods described below are in a way attempts at integrating the broken relations of the person. A method may range from individual healing, group or family to complete the aim of unifying. Here the attention is strictly restricted to the specific methods that are used in pastoral counselling with a blend of theology and psychology.

Christian Counselling

Christian counselling uses a variety of therapeutic approaches, but there is a unity derived from Christ and acceptance of the Bible as an absolute standard. The counselling process can be understood as a three-stage process. A counsellor performs the following functions:

Listens to the counselee.

Helps the counselee gain insight (past vs present, feelings vs behaviour).

Helps the counselee formulate a specific plan of action.

True friendship is built when one person listens to another and shows genuine concern. A warm smile, eye contact and interest shown by every movement are the marks of a caring listener The key to counselling is helping a counselee gain insight by having a balanced view of the past and the present events. For a Christian the past is forgiven (I John 1,9 Phil 3,13-14).The Christian Counsellor must move beyond attention of feelings, however, to deal with behaviour. One way to reprogramme the mind is by studying the Scriptures (Rom 12, 2).

In formulating a new plan, the counselees should make a list of alternatives for dealing with their problems and for being mentally healthy. In helping the counselee formulate a plan, the decision-making process must be given some thought. The criteria for making a right decision are feeling, logic and God's Word.

Biblio Therapy

Biblio therapy is a therapy used for the educated, in which the client starts thinking about related features of his feelings and is of two types. Fiction biography and inspirational literature, offer much in the way of varied expressions of human experience. The mental hygiene type is designed to give useful information to solve human problems and covers, practical principles and facts on adjustment problems. Though this method is more time saving and useful for the pastors, the people may tend to rationalize their problems, while some others think that the readings provide solving of the problems and so he may not enter into a relationship in counselling. Smaller doses of readings are more helpful and these transform behaviour, attitudes, beliefs, and values.

Spiritual Therapy

This is a twelve-step programme oriented for healing addiction, which is the cause of all miseries. This is most effective, widespread, and inexpensive. The term *spiritual* means ' other than material,' a life that is not centred on the material; *therapy that* originated in Homeric Greece first meant spiritual healing. The goal of *spiritual therapy* is thus making whole and it is the fulfilment of a traditional and holistic approach to healing. The strength of the Twelve Steps Programme is that its vision of man is wholesome. It takes individual freedom and responsibility seriously; it admits personal limitations and failures and the need to make reparation. There are exercises of echoing the love of God, hearing sounds, thinking about ones' death and repetition of mantras, etc..."Self Parenting" is twelve steps for the adult children of the alcoholics.

Vision Therapy

John Powel, S.J popularised a method called 'vision therapy' which is a very effective help for anyone to become fully alive. Vision Therapy is a tool first to identify destructive and crippling attitudes, and thus to replace them with healthy and fulfilling ones. From the symptoms that one experiences one tries to go to the cause, to keep in touch with crippling vision. Powel designed the A.V.E.R method for self-help. 1. Identify the activating agent (A),

2.Find out the vision (V), 3.Become aware of the consequent emotional reaction (E), 4.Be aware of the resultant behaviour (R) Vision therapy is a habit breaking and habit making process by replacing the crippling attitude with a positive and liberating attitude. The following are the techniques.

Countering (in order to eliminate unrealistic interpretations of reality, formulate a simple statement of truth or right attitude which replaces the error of faulty thinking or distorted attitude);

Modelling (after identifying the distorted attitude find someone who embodies the vision you would like to have);

Stretching (take the trouble to expand one's awareness of personal potential. It is leaving the comfort zone and acting against inhibitions and fears), and

Praying (there is some one to help us, and this help is available when we ask for it). Correct vision helps us have a positive attitude in everything and we succeed in monitoring our behaviour in the proper direction.

Christotherapy

Christotherapy is a psycho-theological type of reflection to discover the healing power of Christ-meaning in life. It emerged from the personal experience of Dr.Bernard J.Tyrrell who integrated his religious beliefs with his own search for meaning in his life. It is a contemporary expression of the personal stress in Christian tradition on Christ as the physician and the healer of the whole person. In Cristotherapy insight is given through enlightenment; this heals man of existential ignorance, which may be the effect of the personal sinfulness of humankind as a whole. Four types of Christian enlightenment are Existential

Diagnosis, Existential Discernment, Conversion, and Mysticism. There are four corresponding attitudes of heart to these four enlightenments. They are humbleness of heart, listening, "letting be," and "wu wei."

Christotherapy differs from psychosynthesis in that it does not distinguish between a personal psychosynthesis and a spiritual psychosynthesis. Christotherapy is in harmony with the practice of St. Ignatius of Loyola who mirrors in the dynamic movement of his Spiritual Exercises the stages of radical ongoing religious and moral conversion. The goals of four weeks in the Spiritual Exercises are; first week to reform the deformed, second to conform the reformed, third to confirm the conformed, and fourth to transform the confirmed. Thus, Chistotherapy proposes an integration process.

Metaphoric Communication

The change of the activity of the Spirit operates through special words, which address the metaphoric mind, enabling this part of the brain to transform previous word images or metaphors into new ones. These special words or metaphoric communication can take a variety of forms that reflect the multiple dimensions of the biblical conception of the "word." Specifically these dimensions include imagistic, metaphorical words; visual experiences; actions or events; and imperatives. Eight techniques that reflect these varied dimensions are: active imagination, story/parable/dream, reframing, special language patterns, creative memory, action imperatives, affirmations and play.

a) *Active Imagination* It is a visual form of metaphoric communication, in which an imagistic word that a person uses to describe the problem is chosen at first. It is essential that the chosen word must be that of the client, not proposed by the pastor. The pastor then asks the person to close the eyes, and relaxing to increase the inner concentration and imagine a picture of the selected word and visualize it in detail. Follow-up questions may be added to have a detailed exploration such as, what do you see? What colour? Then the pastor asks the person to imagine the image changing it in some way. In the course of the subsequent interaction with the image the person may get blocked and need the encouragement of further vague suggestions from the pastor. Finally, the pastor may facilitate the person's integration of the experience by assigning the practice of visualizing it at home and expressing it in such forms as creative writing, poetry, or art.

b) Story/Parable/Dream The Bible is the best example of communicating truths through the form of stories and parables. A key reason for the effectiveness of stories is that the listener hears someone else or some thing referred to in the story, with no direct reference to him. Milton Erickson's expressions as "A family came to me who..." or "I knew a woman once who..." allow the listener to fill in their own name at the supposed introduction.

c) Reframing Shifting the way the problem is approached so that it is viewed from an entirely different perspective, is reframing. Limiting their thinking to this one frame blinds them to the possibility that there may be other solutions outside the frame. Jesus' whole ministry on earth was itself a radical reframing of our human expectation.

d) Special Language Patterns Bandler and Grinder, who studied these language patterns extensively, state that giving commands within quotations allows the metaphoric mind to actively participate in interaction with the speaker and to choose to what portions of the speaker's communication to respond. Another special language pattern that stimulates the metaphoric mind to participate actively is the use of non-referring words and phrases. E.g. "Ed bought Mary a gift of a dozen red roses," could be rephrased: "Some one did something very meaningful for you on a certain occasion." The latter generalized phrasing would allow Mary to recall a particular event that most fits her needs at that moment.

e) Creative Memory involves drawing upon and reshaping latent resources within families. Persons who come for assistance of any kind have within them the resources they need to accomplish their goals and make the changes they desire. These past experiences are stored and organized in the metaphoric mind. Words are attached to these organizations of experience and serve as labels for them, e.g. 'companionable,' 'happy,' 'confident,' or 'loving' when those labels are spoken in the present, the stored organization of past experience can be recalled.

f) Action Imperatives are the instructions and other homework assignments that resemble biblical language that takes the form of words of command or imperatives in that such instructions require people to actually do something different in their lives. Giving persons a directive to do something different can lead to a change of their world images or metaphors. The repeating of one small part of an experience leads the metaphoric mind to recall the whole experience.

g) Affirmations Goals of personal growth can also be stated as affirmations and directed toward the metaphoric mind. It is important that such statements be worded positively. The metaphoric mind that does not distinguish negations, such as "I will not be shy and not stammer," points the metaphoric mind toward the personal goal of being shy and stammering. The best form is a positive "I am learning to...." beginning phrase followed by a succinct statement of a goal, such as ".... to speak freely and with confidence." Repeating it many times while visualising a detailed image of you doing the goal behaviour increases the effectiveness of affirmation.

h) Play Actually all the techniques described above are creative plays but here more specific are child games or active physical games such as volleyball etc... The imagination is also stirred by playful expression in such creative activities as painting, story writing or music.

Faithful Companioning

Schlauch explains that the power of healing in pastoral counselling is because of *faithful companioning*. The root metaphor drawn from NT passages is related to that of *collaborative translating*. *Faithful companioning* refers to the pastoral counsellors fundamental commitment to be present with and to the person in his/her experiencing regardless of what unfolds. *Collaborative translating* represents the pastoral counsellors recognition that all of what unfolds in the ongoing process of care, will be experienced and interpreted by the participants in different ways and that meaningful conversation is the participant's ongoing process of translating one another's interpretation of what is happening in a collaborative way.

We mediate God's presence of the other through the holy regard of the other as Christ. Schlauch has analysed persons and proposes the various ways in how they are suffering and how it could be overcome. There are people who suffer in part because they are alone in that suffering or they have lost or never had faith in the other. They may have lost or never had membership in a sustaining community that holds and supports them. They may have lost or never had hope in the future or they have lost or never had faith.

Faithfully companioning on a particular sensibility given the unique context of the ministry of pastoral counselling/ pastoral psychotherapy. Schlauch also gives the method of pastoral diagnosis. *Pastoral* implies care of the person and *diagnosis* in contrast implies treatment of the disease. Pastoral clinician/counsellor embraced DSM IV-R as a kind of clinical scriptures. In the primary step, diagnostic variables examine the client's presentation in terms of the dual forces of the *self* and *suffering* and the three domains of *content, affect* and *action*. *Content* refers to cognitive, ideational dimension of a person's experience circulated and conveyed verbally. *Affect* is an area of emotions and feelings, and *Action* is what is enacted and expressed in patterns of behaviour. The next step is formulating goals, after having maintained a good relationship and analysis of the problem. Establishing a course of intervention is important for the maintenance and continuity of the set goals.

So in pastoral counselling, as a psychologist-theologian-ethicist in conversation involves listening, interpreting, and translating the client's report of his experience into a variety of language games as well as engaging the client in light of one's various understanding. As a psychologist, one may identify character structure, strengths, recurrent conflicts, deficits, and symptomology. As a theologian, one may identify how the other may be denying God's presence, action and participation in unfolding events and replacing God in mistakenly presuming the wisdom, authority, and responsibility to act independently of God. As an ethicist, one may seek to discern the client's and one's own sense of responsibility.

Healing or curing of the mind is not caused by a clinician's/pastoral counsellor's extra human power, which leads a client to feel perfectly understood. Rather it is occasioned by experiencing the fluctuating, approximate presence of a sinful but well-intentioned human being who mediates God's love and forgiveness by *faithfully companioning* and *collaboratively translating* what unfolds in fluctuating and approximate ways. Healing comes only because of a counsellor's sincere attitude i.e., "when a suffering person experiences the clinician's commitment, acceptance, hope as those virtues are present in who and how they are in their pastoral clinical attitudes." Thus Schlauch concludes that pastoral counselling heals through the pastoral counsellor's clinical attitude through faithful companioning.

Partnership Pastoral Counselling

John Sullivan presents *partnership pastoral counselling* in the appendix of the book *Pastoral Counselling in a Global Church*. The pastoral counselling model of relationship, healing, prevention, and creative stimulation has been foundational to the workshops and retreats and their co-ordination. This model is multi-dimensional. It begins with *invitation*, develops in a *situation*, is focused through *orientation*, and bears fruit by *reflection*. Each workshop or retreat seeks to be a life process itself, a moving circle, a recreating sphere of interrelating people, experiences, hopes and creative insights. This life process is compared to an apple. Its skin *invites*, the pulp is the experience of the participants- the *situation*, the *orientation* is provided by the partnership team and finally *reflection* like seeds open up future invitation and personal initiative are integral to life giving pastoral counselling on both individual and group levels. Orientation is the dimension of these pastoral counselling models in which the partnership team is most active and more in dialogue with the participants.

Inclusion, empowerment and partnership are some of the fruits of a creative pastoral counselling process; they seem to be the indicator of the movement of God's Creating Spirit among people becoming community. This is the movement of creative pastoral counselling within a culture, across cultures. Pastoral counselling is a creative relationship between people, bringing forth new life and partnership pastoral counselling through invitation, situation, orientation, and reflection becomes one expression of this relationship.

Interdisciplinary Approach

The Chalcedonian pattern, which Hunsinger uses in his work, has been derived from Barth's theological use of it, even though he himself did not apply it to the interdisciplinary questions of pastoral counselling. The analogies Barth is entering here are between the use of the Chalcedonian pattern in understanding the central case (the Incarnation) and its use in understanding other cases.

As applied to the interdisciplinary questions of pastoral counselling, the pattern undergoes certain modifications that distinguish it from the form it takes in Barth's discussion of the Incarnation as well as from the notably different form it takes when he discusses the relationship in human nature between body and soul. In particular, the closer specification of what it means to speak of two terms being related "without separation or division" differs significantly in each case. For the Incarnation it means a mysterious relationship of hypostatic union between Jesus' deity and his humanity. For human nature it means a natural or creaturely union between soul and body. For the questions of pastoral counselling, it means a form of interdisciplinary approach that is at once contingent and ad hoc. The theological and psychological interpretation exists without separation and division, because the complex phenomena they seek to interpret are often intertwined in experience.

Psychological healing or well-being can thus be interpreted theologically as pointing by way of analogy to that more ultimate form of well-being attested by faith as salvation. By interrelating theological and psychological materials in this way, without reducing either to the other but allowing each to make its own distinctive contribution to the therapeutic process a new interdisciplinary approach to pastoral counselling as a ministry of the church has emerged.

Pastoral Family Therapy

Douglas Anderson defines Pastoral Family Therapy as, "an organized, purposeful therapeutic intervention aimed to assist a family to change - under the power of the Holy Spirit." This therapy combines *right* and *left* brain activities.

a) The *right brain aspects,* centres in therapists relying upon their own metaphorical resources. The right brain dimensions centres in therapists so fully trusting their God as their own in most metaphoric resources that they provide family members with powerful experiences that release their abilities to trust themselves.

b) The *left-brain dimension* is expressed through a systematic *conceptual framework* and a *systematic intervention methodology.* The left-brain dimension tells how to think and do family therapy. The therapy will have a purposeful direction, which increases the therapist's self-confidence and the family's confidence in the therapist. This enables them to set goals.

+ Conceptual *framework* needs to answer four questions, namely; What is a family and how does it function effectively? How does a family malfunction? How does a family change in order to restore effective functioning? How can family change be facilitated by therapeutic intervention?

+ *Systematic intervention methodology.* In this doing dimension the family therapist performs five types of activities. They are: joining the family as a temporary tough effective member, assessing the family's problems, planning and contracting with the family for change, implementing the plan for change and leaving the family while helping them integrate the changes made.

Curran's Method

Father Charles Curran's method of pastoral counselling focuses mainly on values and the integrity of the human person. In this "skilled process" one should have productivity of language, language of affect and cognition, discriminating awareness, adequate self-symbolism, personal values, symbols and insight etc... He considers the grouping for "specific symbols" adequate to a person's immediate emotion-charged situation and is therefore one of the main aspects of the counsellor's skill, which consists of a triple process;

1. The client's own confused and mixed up effort to express himself in the emotion-charged language of affect.

2. The counsellor-therapist's striving to understand this language and to respond in a more adequately symbolic or cognitive form.

3. The client's hearing this, analysing it in relation to his own affect-cognitive state and allowing that it either does or does not "fit."

To look more precisely at the responses, Curran has formulated the Emotion-Insight-Choice Diagram. In the beginning of the counselling session people's statements which are often negative can be represented in the bottom vertical line. Mixed with negations and conflict and confusions that are usually some what positive, at the top of the vertical line. The counselling process might be seen as the swirling motion mounted in E-I-C Cross.

By intensifying the negative situation the counsellor creates a misunderstanding which forces the client to explain it further is the procedure usually used in this method. But when the client expresses a strong negative emotion, it has to be exactly shared and understood by the counsellor. But a problem in positive attitudes can be missed when it is surrounded by a great number of negative expressions. After analysing the emotional state the method proceeds from inner view to interview, so to speak. "Insight and choice" include new plans and achievements. Towards the last part of an interview, insights fuse into new plans.

Clinebell's Shepherding Model

Howard Clinebell in his Basic *Types of Pastoral Counselling* presents a group of pastoral counselling techniques as an outcome of the revised model of pastoral counselling. The five ideas of the older model are structured counselling interview, client-centred method, insight as central goal, concepts of unconscious motivation and childhood roots in shaping literature and the approach of pastoral counselling in its inception especially in the 1940s and 50s. But the revised model did not stick on to these principles as a monolithic one; rather flexibility and more choices led pastoral counselling to another level.

The older model emphasized healing (insight counselling) with secondary attention to guiding. The revised model aims at utilizing all four strands; namely healing, sustaining, guiding and reconciling of pastoral care tradition. Each function has its counselling aspect in each in a one to one or small group relationship, which is used to help people handle problems constructively and improve their relationships. In emphasizing sustaining, guiding and reconciling as well as healing, it moves toward a shepherding (or pastoral) model and away from a predominantly medical or psychotherapeutic model. A diagrammatic presentation of the new model is given.

Pastoral care function	Historical expression	Contemporary Counselling expression
Healing	Anointing, Exorcism Saints and relics Charismatic healers	Depth counselling Pastoral Psychotherapy Spiritual healing
Sustaining	Preserving, Consoling, Consolidating	Supportive counselling Crisis counselling
Guiding	Advice, devil craft Listening	Educative counselling Short term decision making Marriage counselling
Reconciling	Confession, Forgiveness Disciplining	Confrontational counselling Super ego counselling Marriage counselling Existential counselling

Strategic Pastoral Counselling

SPC is a brief, structured counselling approach that is explicitly Christian and that appropriates the insights of contemporary counselling theory without sacrificing the resources of pastoral ministry. The term strategic emphasizes the fact that this approach to counselling is highly focused and time limited. Six characteristics of this model are particularly important (BENNER, *Strategic pastoral counselling*).

Counselling can be brief (i.e., conducted in a relatively few sessions) or time limited (i.e., conducted in an initially fixed number of total sessions) or both. SPC is both brief and time limited working within a maximum of five sessions. SPC is bibliotherapeutic. The Bible itself is of course, a rich bibliotherapeutic resource, while there are other sources like the books that range from devotional to inspirational literature for practical self-help, it is holistic. The various "parts" of a person (i.e., body, soul, spirit, heart, flesh, etc.) are never presented as separate faculties or independent components of a person but always as different ways of seeing the whole person. The structure of SPC is what makes the brief nature possible. Each of the sessions has a clear focus and each builds upon the previous ones in contributing to the accomplishment of the overall goal. It is also spiritually focused. As used in biblical anthropology, the heart lies at the centre of our personality and is the point of the integration of our being. The crucial thing to realize in learning to discern the presence of the spiritual is that our spirituality emerges and manifests itself in the broad context of life experiences, not merely in some subset of religious experiences. Focusing on spiritual matters should not be understood as merely watching for opportunities to shift the conversation to religious topics. The focus of SPC should be on spiritual realities and not on religious behaviour.

The three stages of SPC can be described as encounter, engagement, and disengagement. Counselling is not something one does *to* another person, rather it is something one does *with* another person. It is an encounter of two persons who join together in "dialogue relationship," and do so to the end that one might be of help to the other. In **the encounter stage** the following steps are done:

1. Joining and Boundary Setting

Joining involves putting the parishioner at ease by means of a few moments of casual conversation. One way the pastor can do this is by noting similarities between his or her experience and that of the parishioner. Preliminary conversation of this sort never takes more than five minutes and can usually be kept to two or three minutes. Boundary setting involves the communication of the purpose of the first session and if the pastor has not already done so, the time frames for the session and the rest of the work go together.

2. Exploring Central Concerns and Relevant History

The invitation to the parishioner to tell the pastor what brought him or she in, at the present time is an important transition point in that it leads to the person's story. This should be recorded during the session or afterwards. As the parishioner begins to tell the story, the pastor's job is to listen. After hearing an expression of present concerns, the pastor will usually find it helpful to get a brief historical perspective on both these concerns and the person. Ten to fifteen minutes may be spent exploring the development of the concerns and the person's efforts to cope or to get help with him.

3. Conducting a Pastoral Diagnosis

The pastoral diagnosis must be primarily related to the spiritual focus of pastoral counselling. Thus the diagnosis in the first stage involves the assessment of the spiritual well being of the person, while this is intimately connected with his psychological well being. Malony's eight dimensions of *Religious Status Interview* is a good tool for the diagnosing purpose. The dimensions are: 1. Awareness of God; 2. Acceptance of God's grace; 3. Repentance and responsibility; 4. Response to God's leadership; 5. Involvement in the Church; 6. Experience of fellowship; 7. Ethics and 8. Openness in faith.

4. Achieving a Mutually Agreeable Focus for Counselling

The identification of the primary focus naturally leads to a formulation of goals for the counselling. These goals will some times be quite specific but will also be rather broad at times. In contrast to other counselling approaches SPC does not formulate concrete, observable goals.

This second stage is the heart of the counselling process. The work of this stage may begin at the first session. If the full five sessions of SPC are employed, the stage normally provides the structure for sessions 2, 3 and 4.The major tasks of the engagement stage are the exploration of the person's feelings, thoughts and behavioural patterns associated with the central concern and the development of new strategies for change. In this second stage pastor and parishioner stand side by side facing the concerns brought by the person seeking help.

1. Exploring feelings

To acquire an empathic understanding is the best starting point. The goal in the first few sessions of listening to and responding with empathy to the feelings of the one seeking help is not to change them but to facilitate the expression. Once the feelings are accepted and owned, then the person is in a much better position to decide how to respond to them.

2. Exploring Thoughts

Faulty thinking causes and perpetuates problems. SPC sees both thought and feelings as important. Many cases of pastoral counselling originate in negative and misconstrued thinking that is not checked. In such cases turning them to a new perspective in the light of Christian thought is necessary. It is in this phase that SPC uses Scripture most appropriately.

3. Exploring Behaviour

In this final task of the engagement stage the pastor examines what the person is doing in the phase of problem identification and together with the parishioner begins to engineer changes in behaviour that may be desirable. Sometimes the pastor may resist telling the parishioner the changes that he has to make. The aim of this phase is to identify changes that both the pastor and the parishioner agree are important. These tasks require wisdom and dependence on the Holy Spirit for guidance. It is important to set concrete and realistic behavioural goals. This further concretises the plan and greatly increases the chances for its success. This forward movement must be in small steps rather than in one giant and unsuccessful leap.

The Disengagement Stage- The God who is discovered to have been present in the moments of deepest pain, confusion, and despair is a God who does not depart at the end of the fifth session but will continue to be mercifully present as the parishioner goes on in life.

1. Evaluating Progress and Assessing Remaining Concerns

This can begin in the previous sessions. It is advisable to have a break of several weeks before the final session.

2. Arranging a Referral

If significant problems remain at this stage, the last couple of sessions should also be used to make referral arrangements. Ideally this is to be discussed in the second or third session. No counsellor is able to help every one who seeks his help. Again when further referral is required he needs to be aware of the resources. This help may take place in the form of financial counselling, tax advice, legal counsel, or medical or psychological consultation, assessment, and treatment. Pastors should not assume that they are appropriately qualified to handle all the problems. Preparing the parishioner for a referral is also important. He or she should be sent to one in whom he or she has confidence. The failure to refer at the proper time may cause problems and distort his or her personality.

3. Terminating Counselling

Most often the pastor and the parishioner agree that there is no further need to meet and this is the terminating procedure. He or she may have experienced a kind of acceptance or even emotional intimacy in the counselling experience and the gratification of such needs are not the best way of helping a person. Some times the pastor may be tempted to extend the sessions, but it is good to finish the counselling sessions as agreed in the initial session by both parties. The exception to this rule may occur when the parishioner experiences stress or crisis. In such cases further sessions can be again set up for crisis management. Many of those in need will see their minister as a competent, trusted shepherd and will ask him to walk with them through their struggle, pain, or confusion. But, as noted by Clinebell, "If a pastor lacks the required skills, such persons receive a stone when they ask for bread."

VII. GENERAL METHODS

Besides the above-mentioned methods of pastoral counselling there are some psychotherapeutic methods that are mostly used in pastoral counselling. One can see these methods immediately taking effect in a pastor's task. Some of them are as follows.

1. Transactional Analysis

Eric Berne has developed a theory called TA in which, structural analysis, is a valuable tool when used by the pastor who has neither the training nor the time to do long-term intensive therapy. It is designed for working with individuals and can be introduced during the last fifteen minutes of the initial session.

a) TA as Individual Therapy

The use of Structural analysis, immediately gives the counselee some confidence that he is going to learn to control his life in more satisfying ways and with less conflict because he has gained a measure of autonomy. Frequently, with as few as three to eight interviews, the counselee begins to receive the sense of awareness, spontaneity and intimacy. This is not to imply that all problems can be solved rapidly, but only to state that the initial counselling process can be immediately effective; the tools learned in a brief period can have value for the balance of one's life. Structural analysis is a way of analysing the structure of personality. It is a process of identifying and separating what Berne calls the parent, adult and child ego states which are phenomenological realities of every personality. An ego state is a system of feelings, which motivates behaviour patterns related to a given subject. The purpose of Structural analysis is to strengthen the adult, so that it can regulate and mediate the parent and the child and be an executive of personality.

There is no hard and fast way for an initial interview but the usual one is to greet the person with a "Hallo" and observe what happens next while getting his or her name, address, referral resources etc... After this some speak naturally while others wait for the turn of the therapist to break the ice. Any way this is a free session in which the therapist learns the ego states. Successfully terminating an interview is a skill that is important and often developed only in practice. "We can continue this next time" or just looking at the watch, should suffice. But it should not hinder the client. A valid exception to maintaining a firm 50 minutes to an hour would be in case of suicidal or homicidal persons or those exhibiting severe schizophrenic symptoms.

The OK positions are a useful tool for sorting out the games one plays. Knowledge of them is vital for the pastor who wishes to understand his relationship to the counselee. Games are played by the child from the inner conviction of "I am OK or I am not OK". There are four basic convictions: I am OK, I am not OK, You are OK, and You are not OK. These convictions lead to the following possible combinations between the persons, viz.,

I am (we are) OK you (they) are OK (intrinsically constructive)

I am (we are) OK you (they) are not OK (intrinsically paranoid)

I am (we are) not OK you (they) are OK (intrinsically depressive)

I am (we are) not OK you (they) are not OK (intrinsically schizophrenic).

The term OK is an adult term, a sort of middle of the road term, which says the person is neither great nor "not great", but nevertheless, is OK. It is a worthy goal towards which the counselling pastor works, feeling that someone, who rejects the church, is nevertheless OK. Pastors who decide to help others in counselling by structural analysis must be aware of their own ego states, so that knowing from which ego state they are speaking, they are able to estimate its effect on the counselees.

There are different phases of treatment, which consist of mainly three things: establishing a relationship, working through, and termination. *Establishing a relationship* — It is the beginning phase of the treatment, where the client receives some information about TA, and that his problem being understandable his pain can be alleviated. They obtain specific information by asking pointed questions. In some cases however, they take a more active role and interrupt, encourage and comfort. The therapist can decide to refer a client to some other person or situation for *Valid* and *Game* reasons. *Working through-* this middle phase begins when a working relationship has been established between client and the therapist. Attitudes and values, symptoms and defences, feelings of security and esteem can be dealt with during this period, all within the context of the contract. *Termination-* The third phase may be temporary interpretation or it may be permanent, accidental or a co-operative plan, or an autonomous decision by the client alone.

b) TA in Group Therapy

TA can be used in individual therapy, but much of its power comes from its use in groups. Preparing a client before he enters a group is important. Groups are homogeneous and heterogeneous. Many clients prefer evening groups and usually meet once a week for an hour and a half. In institutional care they could meet weekly, semi-weekly or daily. Traditionally, groups are made up of eight members that a therapist can observe well. There are open-ended groups and groups for specified number of weeks. Each need of the member is to be considered individually so that the group work can be effective. It is advised to have at least one interview with the clients before they enter a group. Additional information of the time and beginning and end of the sessions is to be given. Good TA therapists are in the business to cure people, and not merely to make them feel comfortable. Every one who enters the group draws up a personal agenda, which Berne calls provisional group image. It is the image or fantasy of what the group will like and how the members will transact with each other. A basic technique to provide that "some thing better" is to focus on contracts that have been established in a previous private session or in the group itself. In a marathon group, these contracts and the steps involved are written out in large sheets of paper and fastened to the walls or curtains. They thus become a referral point that serves to focus their clients' energies.

About ten minutes before the end of a group session, especially if some one is new to the group and has not spoken, a therapist may direct an open ended question like "Is there any thing you would like to say?" As a general rule the meeting should finish on time. Private conversations with some members after others have gone, is to be caught up in some kind of game as giving up games is a major step toward autonomy. Gaining autonomy is a life long process. When people solve one problem, another crops up. In fact the process of problem solving enhances joy.

2. Gestalt Therapy

The technique of Gestalt therapy revolves largely around two sets of guidelines, which are called "rules" and "games" (*A. LEVITSKY -F.S. PERLS, "The Rules and Games of Gestalt Therapy".*)

a) Some of the *rules* of Gestalt therapy are the following.

+ *The principle of now* – in the communication process it is meant to promote the "now" awareness in the present tense. When a client refers to events of yesterday, last week, or last year quickly direct him "to be there" in fantasy and to enact the drama in present terms *I and thou-* this principle strives to drive home as concretely as possible the notion that true communication involves both the sender and the receiver.

+ *"It" language and "I" language-* through this one learns to identify more closely with the particular behaviour in question and to assume responsibility for it, e.g., instead of "It is trembling," "I am trembling." Changing *it* into *I* is an example in microcosm of many of the Gestalt game techniques.

+ *Use of awareness continuum- it* is the use of the "how" of experience that is absolutely basic to the Gestalt therapy. This leads the patient away from the emphasis on the "why" of behaviour and toward the "what" and "how" of behaviour.

+ *No gossiping-* it is designed to promote feelings and to prevent avoidance of feelings. *Asking questions-* the patient may move from the lazy and passive way of questioning like "give me, tell me" to "How are you doing?" or "Are you aware that?" those that provide genuine support.

b) The following is a brief description of a number of *games* used in the Gestalt Therapy.

+ *Game of dialogue-* The therapist seeks out the splits that are manifested in personality; a major type of it is between top-dog (super ego) and under-dog (passive resistance). The client is asked to have an actual dialogue between these two components of his. The dialogue game can even be applied with various body parts such as left hand versus right, or upper body versus lower or with some significant person.

+ *Making the rounds-* A particular feeling or theme expressed by the client should be faced vis-à-vis every other person in the group. The client may have said " I can't stand any-one in this room." The therapist will then say "OK make the rounds say that to each one of us, and add some other remark pertaining to your feelings about each person." This game is flexible and need not to be confined to verbal communication, but can include touching, observing, frightening etc.

+ *Unfinished business-* Whenever an unfinished business is identified, the patient is asked to complete it. Obviously all of us have endless lists of unfinished business dealings in the realm of interpersonal relations, for instance, with, parents, siblings, and friends.

+ *"I take responsibility"*- In this game one builds on some of the elements of the awareness continuum. The method is that with each statement, you ask the client to use the phrase, "… And I take the responsibility for it." For e.g. "My voice is very soft… and I take the responsibility for it."

+ *"I have a secret"*- This game permits exploration of feelings of guilt and shame. Each person thinks of a well-guarded personal secret. He is instructed not to share the secret itself but to imagine how he feels others would react to it. A further step can then be for each person to boast about what a terrible secret he nurses. The unconscious attachment to the secret as a precious achievement now begins to come to light.

+ *Playing the projection*- Many seeming perceptions are projections. For e.g., the client who says, "I can't trust you," may be asked to play the role of an untrustworthy person in order to discover his own inner conflict in this area.

+ *Reversals*- When the client realizes that overt behaviour commonly represents the reversal of underlying or latent impulses, the therapist uses it. E.g. If the client claims to suffer from inhibition or excessive timidity, he will be asked to play an exhibitionist.

+ *The rhythm of contact and withdrawal*- The natural inclination toward withdrawal from contact, which the client experience is to be overcome but as a rhythmic response to be respected. Consequently when the patient wishes to withdraw, he is asked to close his eyes and withdraw in fantasy to any place or situation in which he feels secure. He describes the scene and the feelings there; soon he is asked to come back to the group.

+ *"Rehearsal"*- According to Perls, a great deal of our thinking consists of internal rehearsal and preparation for playing our accustomed social roles. The group therefore plays the game of sharing rehearsals with each other, thus becoming more aware of the preparatory means employed in bolstering our social roles.

+ *"Exaggeration"*- This game is closely allied to the principle of the awareness continuum and provides us with another means of understanding body language. A similar technique is used for purely verbal behaviour and can well be called the "repetition" game.

+ *Marriage counselling games*- The partners face each other and take turns saying sentences beginning with, "I resent you for ......" The resentment theme can then be followed by the appreciation theme, "What I appreciate in you is..." Then the spite theme, "I spite you by..." Or, the compliance theme, "I am compliant by..."

The theoretical and therapeutic core of Gestalt therapy is awareness. Regarding the termination of therapy the client cannot reasonably terminate without evaluating his progress and cannot do this without being aware of his goals. Basically, Gestalt therapy is designed for some one who is dissatisfied with the way he is, and is willing to expend some efforts to be different- or to become more content the way he is. Many of the specific techniques and principles can be applied to less willing patients- children, psychotics and some disordered characters.

Gestalt therapy has a non-interpretive approach to dreams that permit the client to progress at his own pace and find his own meaning in his dreams. Every image in the dream, whether human, animal, vegetable, or mineral is taken to represent an alienated portion of the self by experiencing and recalling the dream over and over again in the present tense. From the standpoint of each image, the patient can begin to reclaim these alienated fragments, accept them, live with them, and express them more appropriately.

3. Neuro Linguistic Programming (NLP)

Sensory receptors and language act as filters for human experience. NLP is the study of these filtering processes and seeks to understand human modelling processes as they are experienced through sensory perception, language and analogous communications.

People don't perceive reality but rather a neurological model of reality and this forms the basis for our model of the world. There are three mechanisms common to all model building activities, generalization, deletion and distortion. Bandler and Grinder call these "universal-modelling processes." Deletion is the process by which selected portions of the world are excluded from the representation created by the person modelling. Distortion is the process by which the relationships, which they hold among the parts of the model, are represented differently from the relationships, which they are supposed to represent. Generalization is the ability to draw conclusions about a class from the particular. There are various models of human behaviour.

a) *Communication categories model-* this model is organized under four preferred representational systems, viz, visual, kinaesthetic, auditory and digital. The other specific areas of behaviour include postural characteristics, body types and movements, lip size, breathing patterns, voice-tonality-speed-tempo, eye elevations in relation to others, rules for looking while listening, stair categories, Meta model ill-formed meanings and accessing cues.

b) *The Meta model* – R.Bandler and J.Grinder work on the Meta Model (1975) as a linguistic tool, extremely used in therapeutic setting. "The Meta Model is a set of eight linguistic distinctions which can be grouped into three categories. The first category, *gathering information*, begins the process of uncovering and exploring specific portions of the speakers' experiences which are missing from his surface structure or which are presented in a distorted form. The questions asked are (a)who, what, where, when, how, (b) can you say that about yourself etc...The second category, *expanding limits*, provides you with tools to assist the speaker in defining and then expanding the boundaries or limitations of his model of the world. This self-exploration assists in gaining more choices in both behaviour and perception. The questions asked are: (c) What stops you? What would happen if you did? (d) Can you think of a time when you did/ did not? The third category, *changing meanings*, continues the process of growth and expansion by exploring with the speaker how he understands himself and his relationship with the people around him and with the world in general. The questions asked are: (e) how do you know/ (f) how does it make you feel that way? and, (g) according to whom?

c) *The Visual model* – it provides us with a format for seeing, understanding and listening and utilizing consistent patterns of observable behaviour. Pupil responses are very accurate indicators of interest. Through eye scanning patterns or accessing cues constructed images/ eidetic images/ constructed speech/ remembered sounds/ feelings/ internal dialogue/ visualization/ taste and smell could be identified. The other accessing patterns include breathing, body posture and minimal cues.

NLP uses different types of concepts and techniques some of which are:

a. calibration- identify minimal cues i.e., breathing patterns, skin tones, voice quality, posture, gestures etc... associated with specific states.

b. Pacing- matching another's behaviour with your own.

c. Leading- changing your behaviour such that another also changes his behaviour.

d. Mirroring- match a specific posture or gesture of another person.

e. Anchoring- attaching a particular cue to an internal state or behaviour. Using an established anchor is called internal cueing while uninternal anchors are naturally occurring ones. The process of anchoring involves: exquisite timing, the internal cueing of internal responses, and S-R behaviour. Anchors are used within a person's conscious awareness and are repeated as often as necessary to ensure they remain installed.

f. Reframing- When a person's representation of an experience is limited by a negative frame, reframes are used. Simple reframes are changing negative statements into positive ones. Reframing assumes that all behaviours are useful and appropriate in some context. A reframe is successful when the person is willing to accept that the reframe is a valid representation of his experience. The six-step reframing procedure includes:

- Determine the behaviour to change.
- Establish communication with the responsible part.
- Separate the behaviour from the positive intention.
- Generate three alternatives that give a positive outcome.
- Ask the party to take the responsibility for choosing a new behaviour in the appropriate context.
- Ecological check.

4. Brief Therapy

Brief or Strategic therapy was an approach rather than a method, which made a departure from classic theories on counselling, and developed as a science and art by the Palo Alto Group, focuses on the process, by which changes in approach toward the problem are made.

Brief therapy is a directive therapy and the therapist makes use of the art of persuasion (match the client without telling anything, imitate the way he sits, talks or pattern of talking) frequently. But the therapist has to maintain a position of neutrality. The approaches that usually produce no effect are: unsolicited lectures, taking a high moral ground, self sacrifice / denial, spontaneity, etc...

Framing interventions alter the view of the problem and therapy helps people to "jump out" of the frames. In reframing, the therapist provides or encourages the development of a new or alternative frame or meaning to a situation, while in reframing the therapist challenges the meaning that that client associates with the situations without providing a new frame.

The pattern interventions alter the doing of the problem, which means the complaints of the client are resolved by altering the patterns of action. This could be done through changing frequency, duration, time, location, intensity, sequence of events, interrupting, assigning or substracting, breaking up any previously whole element into smaller elements, reversing, linking, the occurrence of symptom-pattern to another pattern, etc...

Paradoxical interventions are described as "a contradiction that follows correct deduction from consistent premises" (Watzlawick *et.al.*, 1967). In this process the therapist in a spirit of seeking to help, seems to promote the continuation or even the worsening of problems rather than their removal. Some of these interventions are: a) Symptom prescription- instead of continuing symptomatic or associated behaviours for the time being or to increase them. b) Prescribing, restraining the therapist discourages the patient from changing or denies the possibility that change can occur and positioning – shift a problematic position by accepting or exaggerating that position. c) Redefinition- attempts to alter the meaning or interpretation placed on symptoms and is seen as most appropriate with families possessing some capacity for reflection and insight. d) Escalation- attempts to create a crisis or to increase the frequency of symptomatic behaviour. e) Redirection- is changing an aspect of a symptom. E.g., prescribing particular circumstances for symptomatic behaviour.

Many problems arise due to lack of balance in taking responsibility. Both over responsibility and under responsibility can lead to problems in relationship and problems in behaviour. In brief a therapist's task is to set right and bring a proper balance of responsibility as the solution to this problem.

5. Multimodal Therapy

Arnold A. Lazarus' multimodal therapy is an educational one, which aims at reducing psychological suffering and thus promote personal growth as rapidly and as durably as possible through a "thorough assessment and the systematic correction of problems across the BASIC ID." BASIC ID is seven separate and related dimensions of personality namely Behaviour, Affect, Sensation, Imagery, Cognition, Interpersonal Relationship and Drugs (medication). There are four stages in the multimodal therapy.

a)   Assessment of the client's current functioning according to the framework of the BASIC ID by using certain issues and questions, which take one hour or more. This enables the therapist to determine the client's specific strengths and weaknesses across the interactive dimensions of "personality", and it reveals the degree of self-knowledge in each specific area. A checklist is also given at the end of the initial interview.

b)   Development of the BASIC ID Modality Profile to the definition of existing problems and intervention plan. The BASIC ID chart is seen as a cognitive map, and provides a clear relationship between diagnosis and treatment by integrating the functions of assessment, the setting of objectives, and the specification of therapeutic techniques. By the end of the third session the therapist discusses the necessity of adjustments in one's behaviour. If the client is "tense" the obvious antidote is "relaxation therapy" and if a person is timid and unassertive "assertive training" is called for.

c)   Implementation of the intervention plan.

d)   Refinement- In later sessions, focusing on interventions the client is taught to cope with stress, as the treatment plan is carried out.

6. Rational Emotive Therapy

Hauck makes a brief therapy with RET and he defines brief therapy as a dozen or fewer sessions. The time period can extend from one to twelve consecutive days or one to twelve visits stretched out over a twelve- month period. The brevity refers to the time required by the therapist, not by the client. And the goal of brief therapy is not the complete revamping of the personality but only of those facets which at that time of the client's life are likely to bring his or her feelings to a considerable degree below the neutral line.

RET Brief counselling sessions last no more, no less than 30 minutes. The first session enables the pastor to get an idea of the client's problem. In 90% of the cases, the problem will emerge during the first session. Hauck's timing of a session follows, "after the introductions are over, and I find I am able to get vital statistics in about two or three minutes. I try to get a picture of the problem in the next 10-15 minutes. Counsel for ten or more minutes and wind up in the last minute or two. In some sessions the dynamics are so obvious that instruction can take place five minutes after the meeting starts which gives a solid 23 minutes to teach RET with two leisurely minutes to wind up setting another appointment and giving a home work assignment. Through this method the pastor could visit 14-16 persons a day. But for those clients who wish more time a double session can be given in the future sessions. Instead of meeting these clients every week, it could be scheduled once in every three or four weeks time.

The steps involved in the first session are the following.

Step 1 collect routine data- get the client's name, age, address, phone number, spouse's name, occupation etc...

Step 2 determine the problem, if possible- simply ask "How may I help you?" or "What can I do for you?" During this phase the counsellor listens to the client for problems; let the client talk at this time.

Step 3 ask questions- learn what the problem is and find out who is involved in the problem, and how the client reacts to it.

Step 4 select a problem- most of the people have a number of emotional and situational problems but decide which of his problems is the most distressing one.

Steps 5 formulate the dynamics- make a coherent statement about what is causing the client's distress.

Step 6 educates the client- by talking. Explain the dynamics and the insights, but don't be a preacher.

Step 7 summary and quiz- this is a time to ask the client for a feedback of what the counsellor has been saying.

Step 8 assign a home work- it could also include psychological tests and recommended readings.

Step 9 schedule future appointments- if more sessions are needed decide by saying "I'll have to see you again," or explain the reasons for the next session.

West and Raynold's study describes certain RET principles for pastoral counselling without violating the theological tenets that separate pastoral counselling from secular counselling. The author has reviewed literature on RET and Pastoral counselling and identified five principles as basic to RET theory in Pastoral counselling and they are presented by using the Delphi technique in which the experts vary in their view on each principle. The principles and the study results are:

		A	D	AM
1.	Irrational beliefs are the primary cause of feelings.	23%	23%	40%
2.	People are limited and fallible.	54%	23%	23%
3.	There is no way valid enough for evaluating the worth of people, hence there is no valid use of judging self esteem	40%	20%	40%
4.	There are no pure "needs' or "musts" in life beyond our physical survival needs.	23%	20%	57%
5.	People are best served when they function as long-range hedonists.	23%	54%	23%
	A-agree D-disagree AM- agree with modification			

The author's conclusion is thus, "the one that best reflects the earlier literature review is that there is a lack of agreement on the degree of dialogue between psychology and theology. There is a lack of consensus within the theological disciplines about the theological tenets of pastoral counselling. There is also a lack of consensus on which psychological theory best reflects an accurate understanding of human beings. For psychological and pastoral counsellors there are many schools of thought from which to draw in their understanding of people."

From the review of the literature on the various methods of pastoral counselling one could conclude that there is no unique method. The influences of the various psychological theories have succeeded greatly in the selection of the theories. Interest and feasibility also induced many psychologists like Curran, Cline bell, and Benner who are reputed as pastoral counsellors to use their own method. So finding a single method for pastoral counselling will be of great help to the pastors who counsel despite their ecclesiastical commitments. Because of this it could be said hypothetically, "pastoral counselling should have a specific and well defined method."

VIII. POINTS TO DISCUSS

Every pastor is happy to help a client or a parishioner seeking help. There is no much difference in adopting this attitude of helping others. While a good number of priests has expressed that there is difficulty in beginning a counselling session, experienced priests agree that there is no difficulty in beginning a session with some common talks or beginning with "How are You?" etc... But many firmly agree that counselling has to be done in a friendly atmosphere. It should not terrify the one who comes with a problem. Rather a pleasant way of proceeding into the personality of the person opens his eyes to see what he is and freely allows him to have his own initiative for change. If the counselling relation is diplomatic or strictly official then the client may not open his mind and the pastoral counselling would end up as a failure.

Pastors are of the view that much time need not be set aside for giving advice as their experience proves that thus far it has produced no effect. No one should take counselling to be simply an advice giving session as students perhaps hold it to be. Likewise priests are also aware of their inability to help a person. It is not only the skill and ability of the pastor that produces good results in counselling but the cooperation of the client, together with the grace of the Holy Spirit. Thus they uphold the view that pastoral counselling is not a monologue but a dialogue with two parties, the client a party to God and again a party to the pastor and God.

It is interesting to note that pastors are scarcely aware of including theology and Ethics in pastoral counselling. They are more concerned about the person and the problem that they deal with, and equally conscious about the moral principles and laws binding the Church. The priest by his very call has the moral obligation to stand for values in every aspect of his life. From their experience many priests say that finding the root cause of the problem is the best way to solve the problem and to deal carefully and efficiently with the case will produce better results. They are also very much interested in giving further appointments to a client who is in real need.

Regarding the time spent for counselling most priests say that they should counsel the client according to his need. So they do not give a specific period of time for a counselling session. Some say that it may range from 30 minutes to two or three hours. On these occasions, most priests have to deal mostly with marriage and family problems than with any others. The next score goes to alcoholism, youth, problem children, anxiety etc... priests have a good and positive attitude towards pastoral counselling. They are very much interested in doing counselling despite their heavy priestly schedule. Studies reveal that most of the priests do not have a specific method of doing pastoral counselling. This is very evident from their use of time and response to religious resources. The students (deacons) who are anxiously waiting to be pastors have certain concepts about pastoral counselling. But they too are not clear about pastoral counselling. The common man often responds satisfactorily to the basic norms of counselling: a friendly atmosphere, absence of advice, etc... But a systematic way of doing Pastoral counselling is lacking in their understanding. So, one could conclude the analysis of results. That pastors as well as those aspiring to be pastors have a positive attitude towards pastoral counselling, though they lack a systematic and unique method for doing pastoral counselling.

The study of the survey of literature on various methods on pastoral counselling and the interviews suggests that there is no proper method adapted for pastoral counselling. The literary analysis focuses on the point that they are much from the central i.e., developed countries to the periphery of the third world countries. The majority of studies on pastoral counselling are conducted outside the Asian/Indian setting, and we blindly take those ideas and methods for use in our context. Even in the case of far developed perspectives on pastoral counselling, there is no unique opinion on the method of pastoral counselling. Many differ on various psychological schools, while others emphasise spiritual/ trans personal aspects. A narrow perspective shows that at the early stage of pastoral counselling, there was no clear theory set up, except the goal of helping the parishioner to salvation using the minimum amount of psychological means. But a progressive view could see the reason for the plurality of methods, as a stage of development. Pastoral counselling is a growing field and every psychological branch has something to contribute to this. While some forget the spiritual/ pastoral aspect, some others only emphasise the spirituality, though still some others hold a balanced view. If in the context of Indian literature counselling is very rare, then what about Pastoral counselling? Of course there are some persons who are quite efficient in this field. But compared to the needs of the people it is inadequate. Can one then find some indigenous methods for pastoral counselling? No, this was the result of the analysis of literature on the concerned topic. But there are many who are really aware of the situation and are coming out with their own therapies and treatment procedures.

Pastoral counselling should have a time-limited model. There is no doubt that every priest is a busy person. He is the only consulter in his parish for many official and personal issues. Besides he leads the liturgy and so pastoral counselling is only a part of his pastoral care for which he has to find time. So a priest can never indulge in counselling for long hours for if he does so, many people with other problems may be at a loss. Beside a priest cannot send a person who comes for help within a few seconds. This will not satisfy the person as his problems will remain unsolved. So the timing cannot go to extremes. Thus one could choose about thirty minutes as a standard timing for dealing with a case with brief therapeutic approaches. But according to the severity of the case he could extend the case or not. The results we receive vary on the time aspect. Most of the priests say that sufficient time should be given according to each case. But this is not feasible because of the busy schedule of the priest. In our context some priests make time to counsel people at the same time that they avoid other programmes for long periods of time. Hence it is advisable to have a scientific method for ease and better results.

As in every other counselling session all agree on the friendly atmosphere required for pastoral counselling. During the encountering and engaging sessions, as the counselling progresses the pastor feels with the parishioner by positively responding, accepting his feelings, following his gestures, carefully listening to the client and commenting accordingly etc. This facilitates the counselling process and encourages the client to speak out more openly. The use of the NLP accessing cues is a great source at this time to read the thinking pattern of the client, whether the response is visual or auditory, gustatory or kinaesthetic etc. Analysing the statements with RET principles, the pastor can find out whether they are logical and rational arguments or simply fault finding. By using the TA structural Analysis a pastor can identify from which ego state the client is speaking and in which state he is responding. Thus in this counselling session a priest could use a variety of therapeutic counselling means to diagnose the problem as well as to guide the client to take a real step for change.

Most people dislike receiving advice, through they are interested in advising others. In the counselling session one should bear in mind that advice has to be avoided. This does not affect the client and the client too is aware of it. But the guidance must provoke the client to take active steps to solve the predominant problem, which causes all others. So setting goals for change and choosing the problems to be resolved are important and must be done by a joint effort rather than merely lecturing on some problem and its history and the effects etc... The results of the study adhere to the theories of counselling on this point.

Most of the priests are interested in giving another session after the initial session. A five-session plan is the best method for doing pastoral counselling. The simple session for 30 minutes to three hours will not be beneficial as compared to the five sessions that are charted periodically. A study by Freud and Russell, says, the delay between the initial and next session was not related to the client rating of the counsellor. So if a priest gives such a long period for each of the four sessions to come, the result has to be analysed in our context. Too much delay may make the client feel that the pastor is not concerned about his problems. So after the initial session the next few sessions of entering into the real counselling process can be done without much delay, while the last session can be done 2 or 3 months after the fourth session. This will help the client to make a review of his life and the decisions taken, and how far they are executed. But in the Indian context one cannot think of a systematic process of doing this. Here we are available and expected to counsel arranging appointments for the later sessions.

While doing the counselling a pastor has to be aware of integrating the religious resources in pastoral counselling too. This is the theological content and presence of the Holy Spirit and salvation of the soul that make the counselling process pastoral. In a simple way the counselling done by the pastor could be termed pastoral counselling, merely due to the fact that a pastor does it. When a pastor does counselling surely he will speak about God, prayer or some examples from the Bible or saints or from his own life etc. Thus there is a clear and marked difference between pastoral counselling and other counselling. Regarding the results most of the priests are not aware of this fact, though they use these resources in counselling. This may be because in their thinking the theology in use is systematic theology or theological concepts by eminent theologians etc.

Regarding the counselling occasions most of the priests agree that marriage and family problems are the first issues that they confront. It is quite common that family adjustments are issues that are more than other problems. The Church has an important role in marriage, and children as well as parents have more access to the Church through Sunday worship, other prayer gatherings, pious associations, Sunday class, seminars etc. For the Christians the Church is the place where they gather, showing fellowship and get a feeling that they are accepted and recognized. The need for socialising is also satisfied here. So when a problem occurs in the life of one of the faithful it is usual to draw the attention of the priest. If a pastor has no personal relationship with each and every member of his parish community, this is a real fact. In our context there are many parishes with more than 1500 families. For a priest to know all the members of his parish is a painstaking job. So here, when people come with problems the priest usually searches for their background, family, relations with others etc but this can go wrong because of second hand information. Besides family problems a pastor usually faces other problems like youth and adolescent problems, alcoholism, anxiety and stress, religious issues etc. In a way every problem of the faithful is a case for pastoral counselling. Thus there are many unclassified problems which claim the attention of the pastor in a general sense.

Now one can also see issuing, a general method or model that can be adapted for pastoral counselling. A

Classical method of counselling can be accelerated as; 1.Reading character, 2.Setting up counselling, 3.Confession and interpretation, and 4.Transforming of personality. These are the practical steps from Rollo May's *Art of Counselling*. In the first stage the counsellor observes the client, his signs, dress, movements, facial expression, voice, family set up etc. While in the second stage the counsellor makes contacts and establishes a rapport. Here empathy in language is important. In the third stage the person pours out his heart and interpretation becomes the task of two persons. If needed tests are conducted and a number of interviews are set up, while in the last stage the counsellor suggests something, here he is aware of the futility of advice, and presents constructive alternatives and creates a function of understanding. The influence of empathy here, will reveal good results.

Clinebell presents a short term counselling in his book *Basic Types of Pastoral counselling*. He begins with a question "What approach is most helpful in a one-to-five interview?" The methods that he suggests are as follows:

1. *Listen intensively and reflect feelings (U response)* - This is an important concern of one- interview counselling as W.E. Oates said, and the pastor has to give 2/3 to ¾ of time for concentrated listening.

2. *Use questions carefully to focus on conflict areas rapidly (P response)* - Here the pastor ask questions aiming at key issues; this is another speciality of the short term counselling. Here a detailed picture and history are not important but the focusing on the problem and its solution.

3. *Help the person to review the total problem* - Under protracted stress it is possible to confuse the real nature of the problem and lose sight of the resources for coping.

4. *Provide useful information* - The pastor explains the problem and its nature. It is an educative element to improve the client's condition.

5.*Focus on the major conflict problem or area of decision with the aim of clarifying viable alternatives* - We saw this already in the previous part of our discussion. Providing alternatives is a helping hand for the client to choose an option.

6. *Help the person to decide* on the "next step" and then take it, if it will be positive for the well being of the person. If the person needs further time to take a decision it is better to wait.

7. *Provide guidance when it seems useful* – The pastor's knowledge and authority is essential. The pastor can propose consulting others, or himseslf at regular intervals.

8. *Give the person emotional support and inspiration* - this is a positive stroke, a *Captatio benevolentiae*, which encourages the person to sustain in change.

9. *Move into long-term counselling* - if the above method is not sufficient.

Clinebell's method too falls in the above category as setting the background, entering into, making agreed decisions to change and executing it.

The Strategic pastoral counselling is a good model for doing pastoral counselling. It is very well suited for priests; rather it includes the concepts of counselling as well as pastoral counselling. It blends theology and psychology, and is in the context of 'pastoral' and 'counselling.' Some of the special features of this model are: Brief and time limited, Bibliotherapeutic, Wholistic, Structural, Spiritually focused and Explicitly Christian. Bennerian insights in the field of Psychology, lead to the formation of such a good method, which has not left out any part of pastoral counselling. So a predominance of religion in a way balances the theological concepts with a psychological one by equal sharing, besides the special features of including all areas of counselling and theology.

Certain proposals for doing counselling are the following:

Preparation and motivation is an important step in counselling

1.   *Place*- Having a suitable place for talking is a must. A room with a calm atmosphere, away from the telephone, radio, TV, is suitable for it. There should not be too many things inside the room to disturb the client. In a parish setting a pastor's office is the place where they conduct counselling. But this can create disturbances for the person.

2.   *Privacy*- Besides the above-mentioned difficulties the parochial office room lacks privacy; people may come to meet the priest on some business. So another room could be set up for this.

3.   *Confidentiality*- The counsellor should have the mentality of keeping secrets. Pastoral counsellors are well qualified in this aspect, since they hear confessions. A client should feel that this pastoral counsellor will keep his secrets, and this will induce him to open his mind and speak out freely.

4.   *Motivation*- the motivation of both the client and the counsellor is important. The client has to be in a peaceful mind to clearly speak out the whole problem; too much anxiety and feelings are out of place and will

not produce good results. The pastor too has to be patient enough to sit and calmly hear the client.

5.   *Greeting*- In the encounter stage the pastor may welcome the client with respect and a cheerful heart, and either ask the client to sit or show a seat. The initiative for beginning the session has to come from the counsellor. We have seen how every priest is very much interested in helping the client who seeks help, so naturally they will show a welcoming heart for counselling.

6.   *Listen carefully*- The pastor has to show interest in the client. Without too much passivity he should be alert and directive as needed. Looking into his eyes and untied hands, and a cheerful face is a important thing that has to be maintained. Receiving guests and phone calls is to be avoided.

7.   *Encourage the client*- With positive strokes; acceptance, warmth, and rapport are some of the means to do this. The person is more important than the thing. It is the person to be explored and turned to a normal condition, the image and likeness of the person has to be blended accordingly. For this accepting the person without any difficulties and giving due importance to his feelings is important.

8.   *Diagnosis*- the diagnosing tool like *Religious Status Interview* of Malony (1988)can be used. This focuses on eight dimensions, viz., awareness of God, acceptance of God's grace, repentance and responsibility, response to God's leadership, involvement in the Church, experience of the fellowship, ethics and openness in faith. These dimensions and questions concentrate more on spirituality. Though they are applied to the real life situation of the

person and analysed in detail, they lack a starting point
from a normal phase, or existential level. The sole existence
is only because of God, but a beginning from the natural
situation of the person will place him in a normal setting.
So Malony's *Interview* is only a part of the pastoral
counselling diagnostic tool. Another question to be asked
is why the attention of the client should be drawn to
matters that do not concern him. The problem of the
client is to be analysed and guided; for this one should
not complicate matters. If the client does not open himself
up, the pastor could ask questions pertaining to the
problem mentioned in order to provoke him to speak
without any inhibition.

The analysis of the result shows that priests are not
very interested in using theology, ethics and the Bible in
their counselling situation. They focus more on the person
than on theories. But placing these theories in context is
a special talent that a pastor has to achieve to veer the
counselling process to a pastoral nature.

Another problem in using the more Christian and
theological perspective, is evident when a pastor has to
help persons of other creeds. When a Hindu or Muslim
comes to a pastor for help, can we call it Pastoral
counselling? Coming from the pastor this process could
surely be called pastoral counselling. But from the part of
the client who is not a parishioner and neither one of the
faithful it is difficult to answer. But according to me, the
concept of the church with regard to other religions is
much wider today. They are also on the path of salvation,
though not knowing the real path. Helping a person of
another religion is of course a chance for evangelisation,

but that is not our motive, but to help the client. So helping a man of another creed can also be included in pastoral counselling. Another observation to support this argument is that all persons in the given territory of the parish comprise the local church, and the pastor is the spiritual guide of that region irrespective of caste or creed. This wider vision of the Council Fathers enabling one to extend the boundaries of pastoral counselling, while strictly limiting the diagnostic questions to a Christian setting with other people may result in strangeness.

9. *Engagement Stage-* Here the exploring is done at three levels: emotion, cognition and behaviour. This is a time consuming task. This may take a good number of sessions to conduct in the proper way. Benner is not speaking of the ways of doing these. But here a pastor could use various techniques/ methods from different schools of psychology. TA, RET, NLP, Gestalt etc. are only some of them. These approaches have various techniques to handle specific cases. For e.g. systematic desensitisation is a technique that is given for phobias, while aversion therapy and token economy is given for addiction treatment. The Gestalt empty chair exercise is given to persons to cope with their inner self or with others with whom they has some problems. Thus choosing an appropriate technique at this period a pastor can successfully conduct the pastoral psychotherapy. But this is not the major aim of pastoral counselling, but of psychotherapy. A priest is not competent enough to do these processes in a scientific way. But in his counselling sessions, an awareness of these techniques will help a lot, not for treatment but for use at the appropriate time. So in counselling therapeutic measures are not expected while

inclusion off some principles of those approaches is very helpful in pastoral counselling. So in that sense theology and psychology are equally a part of pastoral counselling.

To conclude the discussion, one could say that the presented models are the best fitted for pastoral counselling in the Indian context with certain modifications. By affirming the need of pastoral counselling, the development of an indigenous method is essential. Accepting the western views on pastoral counselling we need to sow the seed of pastoral counselling to sprout up and flourish in our land. Thus by applying these methods, a priest could easily practise the task of pastoral counselling.

IX. TO CONCLUDE

One could conclude stating in general terms that as pastoral counselling does not have a definite method it is up to the pastor to choose a method of his own interest and work with it. But the point to bear in mind is that while applying pure psychotherapeutic means for counselling a parishioner, the pastor should not forget to include the religious resources at hand. He should be aware of the value of time in his pastoral work. He may not be able to spend long hours on psychoanalysis and even on some therapies like TA and Gestalt while being inconvenient means for him, he has to rely on the brief therapies. Foreseeing all these aspects in the field of pastoral counselling Benner has developed a method which is best applicable for pastoral setting i.e., *Strategic Pastoral Counselling*. But certain modifications could be made in SPC especially at the engagement stage by adapting certain techniques of psychotherapeutic counselling as per the result of the diagnosis. Besides these well set up stages and methods, a pastoral counsellor should have certain qualities to carry out these functions. Though every priest is a counsellor, all are not efficient in carrying on this process.

One could define pastoral counselling as an established rapport between a priest who is a leader, sanctifier and counsellor and a person or family seeking help to resolve the problem through exploration, clarification and guidance at the experiential and behavioural levels through a theological perspective. Pastoral counselling cannot have its own identity without the unity of psychology and theology. The aim of pastoral counselling is to lead people to God and for this a pastor uses common psychological methods, which are not so complicated for both pastor and parishioner. The task of the pastor in helping some one is not only restricted to a time bound period, but it is extended through out the ministry of a pastor. His preaching, teaching, leading worship, small community gatherings are the means for keeping his people united in Christ, and dealing with problems of life. Though the priest is not a psychologist he is called to do the work of a counsellor. The advanced knowledge in the field of counselling is not a must, though he should at least know the basics of counselling.

His personality, skills, interest in helping others are important factors of a counselling process. A priest could do the wok of counselling in a church context and this is a peculiar feature of pastoral counselling and could be done at the request of a parishioner who needs help. It is good to conduct with prior appointments, as this will enable both the priest and the person to ready themselves for the counselling process. A priest who has many other commitments in his pastoral life will be really busy with his daily schedule, of prayer, public worship, meetings, seminars, family visits etc. While counselling, the pastor may not forget to include the resources and it usually will not happen, since the priest is the one who is in constant touch with the Bible, prayer, sermons etc which he will surely include. The experience from his life will colour the process, while he avoids advice and sermonising. Today pastoral counselling is a real need, especially in India where therapeutic counselling has not been well established. Many people need the priest counsellor, though they do not really realize it and encourage it. There are many merits in pastoral counselling like the pastor feeling accepted and appreciated, growth in his own spiritual and personal life, his gratuitous service and availability etc.

There are different occasions and different persons a pastor has to be involved with in the process of counselling. He has to meet children as well as the elders, though most of the problems are those of adulthood and adolescence. Some of the common problems that a pastor usually faces are marital and family problems, sickness and healing, depression, low self-esteem, death, suicide, loss of hope, religious issues, financial crisis, mental disorders, alcohol addiction etc... But a pastor is not an expert in any of the above fields to be able to handle them adequately. So if the priest feels that a case is not working out with his own help, he should not fight shy to ask the help of some one who is an expert in the concerned field.

Different methods have been experimented with in psychological counselling to help people in the problems already cited above. They are the psychodynamic (especially the psychoanalysis) behavioural, humanistic and existential, spiritual or transpersonal and mixed approaches. All these approaches in a way have contributed to the development of pastoral counselling. So pastoral counselling is not an entirely new science, established on its own resources rather it is the outcome of existing theories and experimentation.

Our focus is specially to concentrate on a specific method for the stabilising of pastoral counselling. The analyses of literature on various methods which pastoral counselling mostly uses are studied for this purpose. Each approach or therapy relies on one hand on its peculiar nature in offering counselling while on the other hand there is a sense of something lacking. However in general all have some common grounds like establishing a relationship, listening, empathetic understanding, a friendly atmosphere, problem oriented, solution focused and a recheck etc... But among these *Faithful Companioning* means the pastor's fundamental commitment is to be present to the person who needs help, while the *Interdisciplinary Approach* presents a theological and psychological interpretation without separation and division under the Chalcedonian pattern, blending the Barthean insights. Father Curran's major concern was on values and the integrity of the human person. In *Partnership Pastoral Counselling* a model of relationship, healing, prevention and creative stimulation are dealt with, while *Metaphoric Communication* concentrates on eight techniques like active imagination, story, reframing, creative memory etc. But Clinebell's *Shepherding Model* is a classical one in which he emphasises healing, sustaining, guiding and the reconciling actions of a priest and opened horizons in the field of pastoral counselling in his work, *Basic Types of Pastoral Counselling*. Besides the therapies that are in direct relation to pastoral counselling, some other psychotherapeutic means like TA, Gestalt, RET, NLP which are very much used in pastoral counselling are also analysed from their process or stages of working. And what is a common factor among them is the primary goal of helping people, through relationships and proceeding through systematic set ups.

Some of the norms that are applicable and are recommended in the study of pastoral counselling are the following generalisations.

> There should be more opportunities available to the pastors for acquiring the know how of pastoral counselling through seminars, offer of books.

> Dioceses can take active steps to form a department for pastoral counselling.

> Pastoral counsellors can hold occasional gatherings and study certain aspects; like the method of doing the pastoral counselling, its aim, means, resources etc... all of which have to be clearly set up through statements.

> People are to be conscientised on the need and the benefit of pastoral counselling.

> Further researches are to be done in the field of pastoral counselling in the Indian context.

In particular one could also recommend the following:

> existing methods with certain modifications as a model for pastoral counselling.

> Counselling has to be time limited, in a friendly atmosphere, and should avoid advice giving.

> Pastors must have certain skills like empathetic understanding, exploring nature and action orientation.

> Pastoral counselling is a joint action. So the directive method is not suitable, though required for some time.

> Inclusion of theology, ethics and the Bible is necessary.

> Pastors must know the psychological trends and how to integrate the Bible, theology and psychology in the best way possible.

> Knowledge about brief counselling, solution-focused approaches is a help for pastors to do pastoral counselling effectively.

> Focusing on the client's problem is more important than aimlessly moving in circles.

> Experiencing the presence of God as a first party in pastoral counselling.

> All counselling occasions are important in pastoral counselling; hence one should not easily dispense with any of them and eliminate them at will.

In sum and substance one could say that pastoral counselling does not have a method today, and existing methods with certain modifications could be well adapted in India's cultural context. Future research should be directed toward the finding of new method/s that may produce potential effects in the field of Pastoral counselling, in India as well as in a variety of settings outside.

X. FURTHER READING

ALLPORT, G.W., "Preface" in FRANKEL, V.E., *Man's Search for Meaning* (New York : Washington Square Press, 1969).

ANDERSON, D.A., *New Approaches to Family Pastoral Care* (Philadelphia, USA: Fortress Press, 1980).

ARCHER, J., "Counselling College students," in *The Counselling Sourcebook: A Practical Reference on Contemporary Issues* (ed. RONCH, J.L. – STILWELL, N.C.,) (New York: Crossroad, 1994).

ASHLEY, B.M., *Health Care Ethics* (USA: St. Louis) taken from MANALEL, G., *Pastoral Counselling* (Mumbai: St. Pauls, 1999).

ATKINSON, D.J., - FIELD, D.H., "Pastoral Care, Counselling and Psychotherapy" in *NDCEPT*, 81-86.

BENNER, D.G., *Strategic Pastoral Counselling: A Short Structured Model* (USA, Michigan: Baker Book House, 1996).

BOOTZIN, R.R., - ACOCELLA, J.R., *Abnormal Psychology: Current Perspectives* (New York, USA : Random House, 1984).

BRAKE, G., "Panama" in R.J.WICKS - B.K.EASTADT (eds) *Pastoral Counselling in a Global Church : Voices from the Field* (Mary Knoll, New York : Orbis Books, 1993).

CAVANAGH, J.R., *Fundamental Pastoral Counselling: Technique and Psychology* (Milwaukee, USA: Bruce Publishers, 1962).

CHUNKAPURA. J., - THOMAS. M. J., - MANNARKULAM, *Hand Book of Counselling and Psychotherapies* (Kottayam: Sanjivini, 1997).

CLINEBELL, H.J., *Basic Types of Pastoral Counselling* (Nashville: Abingdon Press, 1966).

CRISPI, E.L., - FISHER, C.B., "Development in Adulthood," in *The Counselling Sourcebook: A Practical Reference on Contemporary Issues* (ed. RONCH, J.L. - STILWELL, N.C.,) (New York: Crossroad, 1994).

CURRAN, C.A., *Counselling and Psychotherapy : The Pursuit of Values* (New York: Sheed and Ward ,1968).

ENRIGHT, J.E., "Introduction to Gestalt Techniques" in J. Fagan-I.L Shepherd(eds.), *Life Techniques in Gestalt Therapy* (Harper and Row: London, 1970).

FREUD, R.D., - RUSSELL, T.T., - SCHWEITZER S., "Length of Delay Between Intake Session and Initial Counselling Session on Clients Perception of Counsellors and Counselling Outcomes" *JCP*, 38/1 (1991) 1-12.

FUSTER, J.M., *Personal Counselling: An Integration of Carkhuff's Models* (Bombay : St. Pauls).

GASTONGUAY, D. , in WICKS, R.J., - EASTADT, B.K. (eds) *Pastoral Counselling in a Global Church : Voices from the Field* (Mary Knoll, New York : Orbis Books, 1993).

GENETRIX - ANTONY, *A Report on Psychosynthesis*, (De La Salle University, 1996) 1-12.

GRACIA, T., - KATTIKAT. X., "Brief / Strategic Therapy," An unpublished paper presented for the course of approaches to Individual Counselling and

Psychotherapies, XAICOSY (Philippines: Della Salle University, 1996)1-13.

HAUCK, P.A., *Brief Counselling with RET* (Philadelphia: Westminster, 1980).

HILTNER, S., *Pastoral Counselling* (Nashville: Abingdon, 1981).

HUNSINGER, D.D., *Theology and Pastoral Counselling: A New Interdisciplinary Approach* (Secundrabad : OM Books, 1999).

ICD-10 Classification on Mental and Behavioural Disorders: Clinical Descriptions and Diagnostic Guidelines (WHO, Geneva, 1992) and (Delhi : Oxford University Press, 1994).

JAMES, M., *Techniques in Transactional Analysis for Psychotherapists and Counsellors* (Philippines: Addison-Wesley, 1977).

JONES, S.L., "Ellis, Albert," *NDCEPT*, 337.

KAY, W.K., - WEAVER, P.C., *Pastoral Care and Counselling a Manual* (Cumbria, GB: Paternoster, 1997).

KEITEL, M.A., - KOPALA, M., "Health Counselling," in *The Counselling Sourcebook: A Practical Reference on Contemporary Issues* (ed. RONCH, J.L. – STILWELL, N.C.,) (New York: Crossroad, 1994).

KENNEDY, E.C., - CHARLES, S.C., "Counselling, pastoral," in *The HarperCollins Encyclopaedia of Catholicism*, R.P.Mc BREIN(ed.) (New York, NY :Harper Collins, 1995) 371-374.

KOSEK, R.B. "The Contribution of Object Relations Theory on Pastoral Counselling," *JPC* 50/4 (1996) 373-377.

LANGS, R. , *Psychotherapy: A Basic Text* (New Jersey, USA : Jason Aronson Inc, 1990).

LEVITSKY, A., - PERLS, F.S., "The Rules and Games of Gestalt Therapy" J. FAGAN -I.L SHEPHERD (eds.), *Life Techniques in Gestalt Therapy* (Harper and Row: London, 1970).

LEWIS, B. ,- PUCELIK, F., *Magic of NLP Demystified* (Portland: Metamorphous ,1993).

LMARVELL-MELL, *Basic Techniques Book I* (Portland, USA: Metamorphous Press ,1989).

LOVINGER, R.J., "Religious Issues," in *The Counselling Sourcebook: A Practical Reference on Contemporary Issues* (ed. RONCH, J.L. – STILWELL, N.C.,) (New York: Crossroad, 1994).

MAES, J.L., "Can Pastoral Counselling Flourish in a World of Managed Care?" *JPC* 50/2 (1996) 136-148.

_____, "Guest Editorial," *JPC* 2/50 (1996) 137-138.

MANALEL, G., *Pastoral Counselling* (Mumbai: St. Pauls, 1999).

MARCEL, G., *Therapikal,* (Cochin : Capuchin Psycho Spiritual Centre, 1979).

MEIER, P.D., - MINIRTH, F.B., –RATCLIFF, D.E, *Introduction to Psychology and Counselling: Christian Perspectives and Application* (Michigan, USA: Baker Books, 1995).

MAY, R., *The Art of Counselling* (Nashville, Abingdon, 1964).

NEZIROGLU, F., - YARYURA, J.A.,-TOBIAS, "Obsessive –Compulsive Disorder," in *The Counselling Sourcebook:*

A Practical Reference on Contemporary Issues (ed.) (New York: Crossroad, 1994).

ORNUM, W.V., - MORDOCK, J.B., "Counselling Adolescents," in *The Counselling Sourcebook: A Practical Reference on Contemporary Issues* (ed. RONCH, J.L., -.STILWELL, N.C,) (New York: Crossroad, 1994).

PANIKULAM, D., *Fear of Death and Neuro-linguistic Programming*, V.S.ANTONY (ed), (Delhi: Media House ,1995).

PELTZ, F.D., - BRIZER, D.A., "Counselling HIV/AIDS Patients," in *The Counselling Sourcebook: A Practical Reference on Contemporary Issues* (ed. RONCH, J.L., -.STILWELL, N.C,) (New York: Crossroad, 1994).

ROGERS, C.R., *The Client-Centered Therapy* (New York: Houghton Mifflin Co., 1951).

SALAMON, M.J., "Marriage and Marital Counselling," in *The Counselling Sourcebook: A Practical Reference on Contemporary Issues* (ed. RONCH, J.L., -.STILWELL, N.C,) (New York: Crossroad, 1994).

SCHLAUCH, C.H., *Faithful Companioning: How Pastoral Counselling Heals* (Minneapolis, USA: Fortress Press, 1995).

SHELTON, C.M., *Pastoral Counselling with Adolescents and Young Adults* (New York, NY: Crossroad, 1995).

SMITH, D.E., - SEYMOUR, R.B., "Addictions Counselling," in *The Counselling Sourcebook: A Practical Reference on Contemporary Issues* (ed. RONCH, J.L., -.STILWELL, N.C,) (New York: Crossroad, 1994).

STRUNK, O.C., "Pastoral Counselling," in *Encyclopaedia of Psychology, Vol.6*, A.E.KAZDIN (ed.) (New York,

USA: American Psychological Association & Oxford University Press, 2000) 64-68.

STURGES, J.S., "Family Dynamics," in *The Counselling Sourcebook: A Practical Reference on Contemporary Issues* (ed. RONCH, J.L., -.STILWELL, N.C,).

SULLIVAN, J., "Partnership Pastoral Counselling" in WICKS, R.J., - EASTADT, B.K., (eds) *Pastoral Counselling in a Global Church : Voices from the Field* (Mary Knoll, New York; Orbis Books, 1993).

TAYLOR, H., *Applied Theology 2; Tend My Sheep* (Delhi: ISPCK, 1989).

THEKKINEDATH, L.P., *Dynamics of Personality Development* (Bangalore: Dharmaram, 1997).

TORRALBA, Y.L., -MONTANO, J.R., "Multimodal Therapy: Approaches to Individual Counselling and Psychotherapies," (Philippines: Death Salle University, 1996) 1-25.

VAUGHAN, R.P., Basic *Skills for the Christian Counsellor, An Introduction for Pastoral Ministers* (Mahwah, NY: Paulist Press, 1987).

VEERARAGHAVAN, V., *A Text Book of Psychotherapy* (Delhi: Sterling, 1985).

WALLIS, J.R., "A Theology of Psychotherapy" *JPC 50/3* (1996) 263-272.

WEST, G.F., - RAYNOLDS, J. "The applicability of Selected Rational Emotive Therapy Principles for Pastoral Counselling" JPC, 51.2,1997, 192-197.

WEST, G.F., "The Applicability of Selected RET Principles for Pastoral Counselling," JPC 51/2 (1997) 187-192.

WOOD, N.S., "Inquiry Into the Pastoral Counselling Ministry Done by Women in the Parish Setting," *JPC* 4/50 (1996) 348-356.

WOODWARD, J., - PATTISON, S., *The Blackwell Reader in Pastoral and Practical Theology* (Great Britain, Oxford: Blackwell, 2000).

WORCHEL, S., - SHEBILSKE, W., *Psychology: Principles and Applications* (New Jersy: Prentice Hall, 1986).

WULFF, D.M., *Psychology of Religions; Classic and Contemporary* (New York, NY: John Wiley & Sons, 1997).

ZIEGLER, W.M., "Formal Pastoral Counselling in Rural Northern Plains' Churches," JPC 4/50 (1996) 393-406.